"Young readers will happily fall in line."
—Kirkus Reviews

"Frolicsome and breathlessly paced."
—Booklist

"Eye-grabbing black-and-pink graphics."
—Publishers Weekly

"The whole package is fresh and funny and even philosophical when it comes to values that third-graders understand."
—San Francisco Chronicle

Be sure to read **all** the **BABYMOUSE** books:

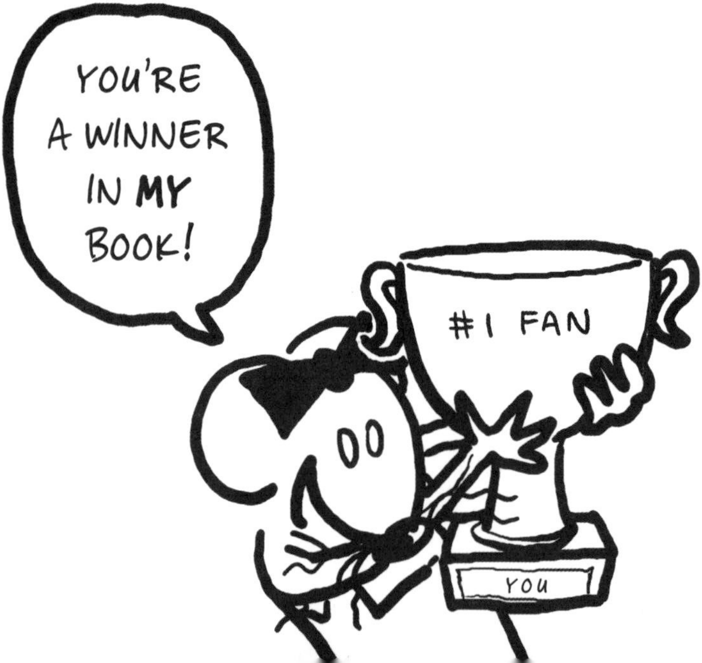

YOU'RE A WINNER IN MY BOOK!
#1 FAN
YOU

BABYMOUSE
SKATER GIRL

BY JENNIFER L. HOLM & MATTHEW HOLM

RANDOM HOUSE 🏠 NEW YORK

YOU'D THINK THEY COULD COME UP WITH SOMETHING MORE INTERESTING TO PUT ON THIS PAGE.

Published in the United States by Random House Children's Books, a division of Random House, Inc., New York.

RANDOM HOUSE and colophon are registered trademarks of Random House, Inc.

www.randomhouse.com/kids
www.babymouse.com

Educators and librarians, for a variety of teaching tools, visit us at
www.randomhouse.com/teachers

Library of Congress Cataloging-in-Publication Data
Holm, Jennifer L.
Babymouse : skater girl / Jennifer L. Holm & Matthew Holm.
   p.   cm.
ISBN 978-0-375-83989-4 (trade) — ISBN 978-0-375-93989-1 (lib. bdg.)
I. Graphic novels. I. Holm, Matthew. II. Title. III. Title: Skater girl.
PN6727.H592 B35 2007   741.5'973—dc22   2006050444

PRINTED IN MALAYSIA

10 9 8 7 6 5 4 3 2 1

First Edition

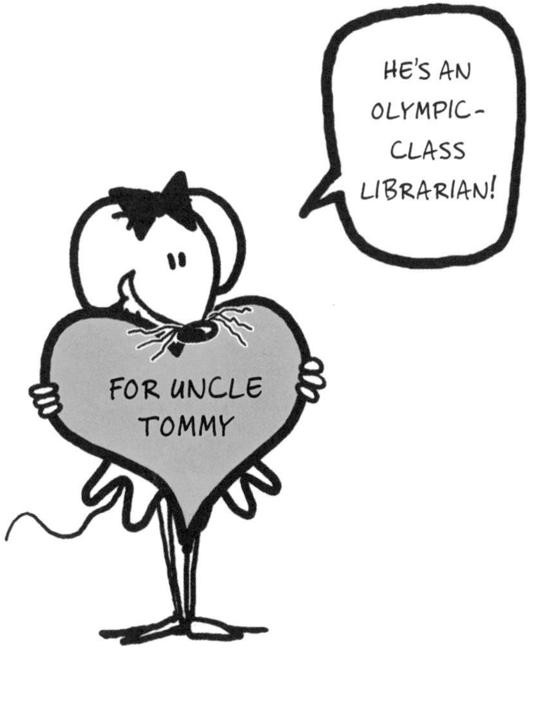
HE'S AN OLYMPIC-CLASS LIBRARIAN!
FOR UNCLE TOMMY

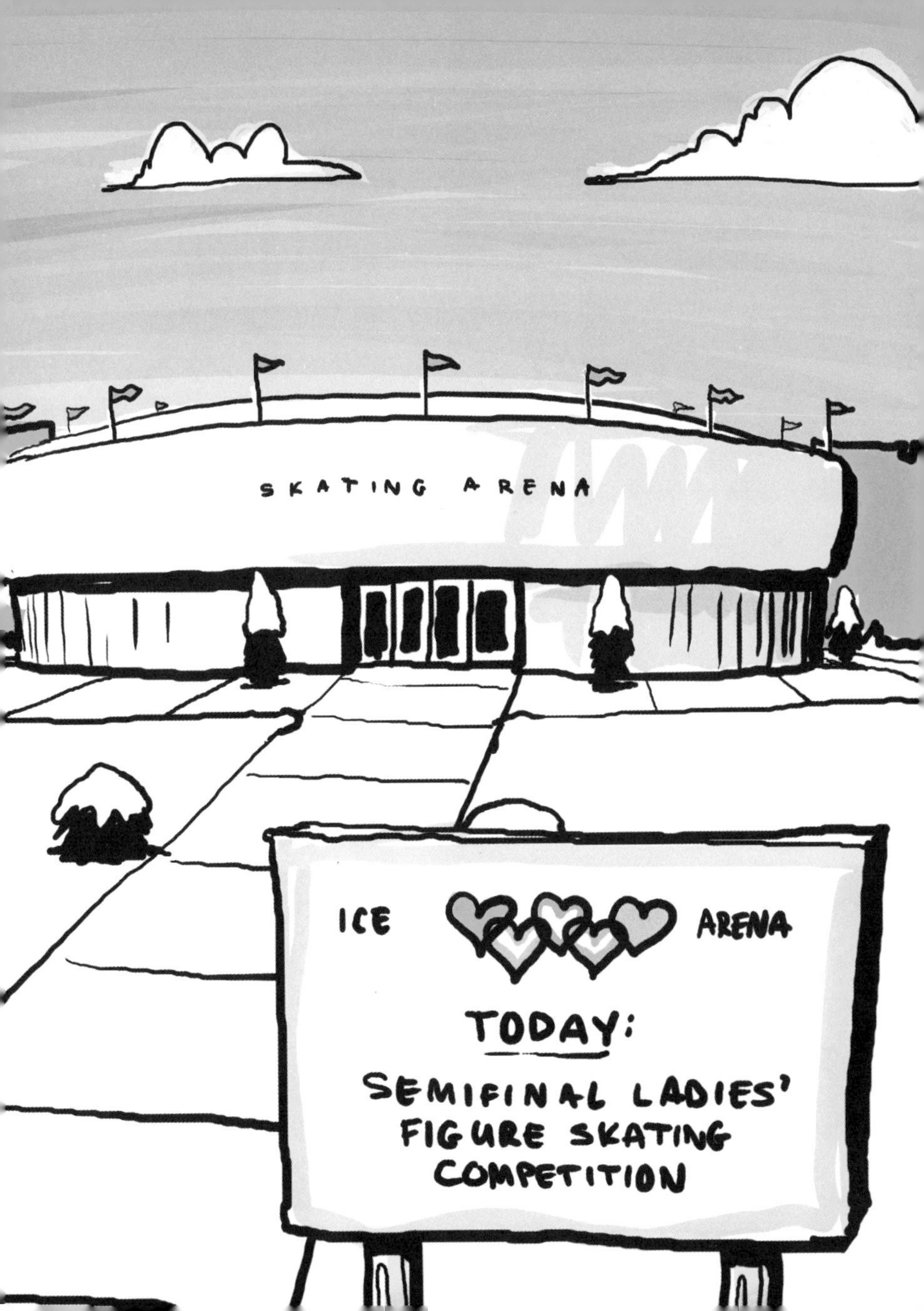
SKATING ARENA
ICE ARENA
TODAY:
SEMIFINAL LADIES' FIGURE SKATING COMPETITION

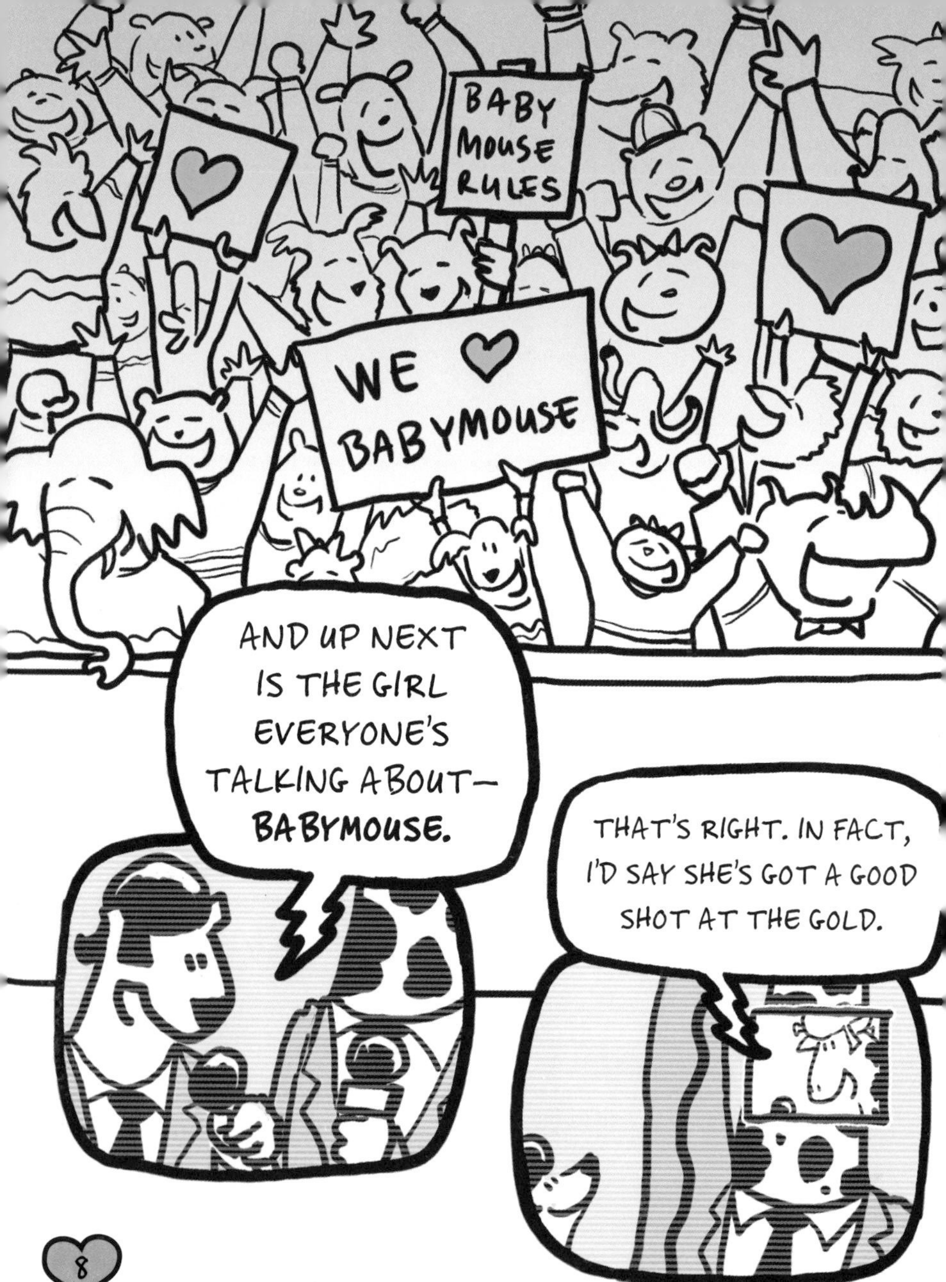
BABY MOUSE RULES
WE ♥ BABYMOUSE
AND UP NEXT IS THE GIRL EVERYONE'S TALKING ABOUT—BABYMOUSE.
THAT'S RIGHT. IN FACT, I'D SAY SHE'S GOT A GOOD SHOT AT THE GOLD.

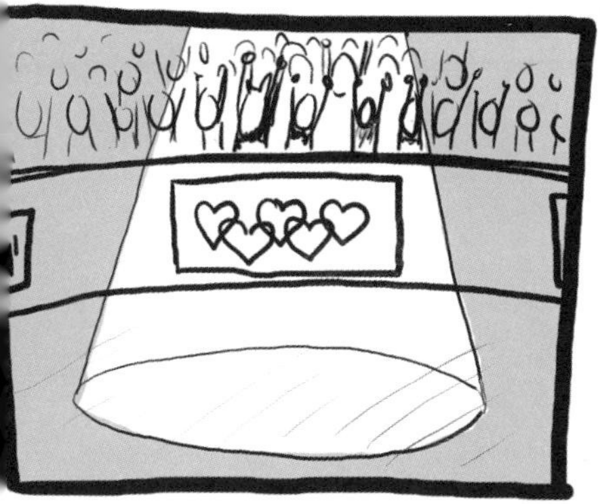

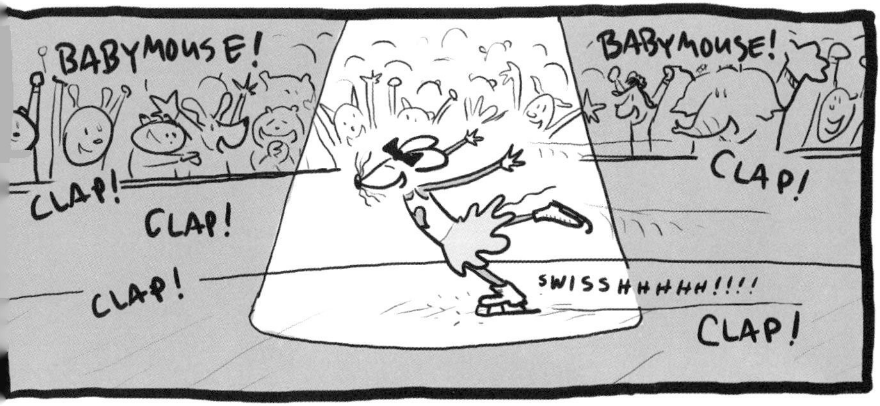
BABYMOUSE!
BABYMOUSE!
CLAP!
CLAP!
CLAP!
CLAP!
SWISSHHHHH!!!!
CLAP!

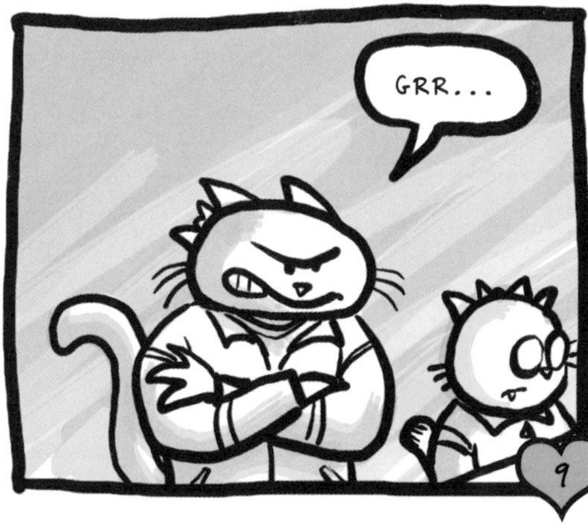
GRR...

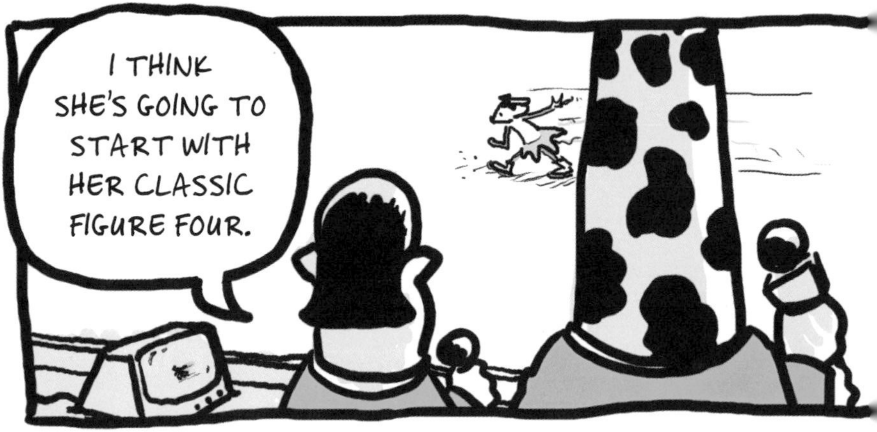
I THINK SHE'S GOING TO START WITH HER CLASSIC FIGURE FOUR.

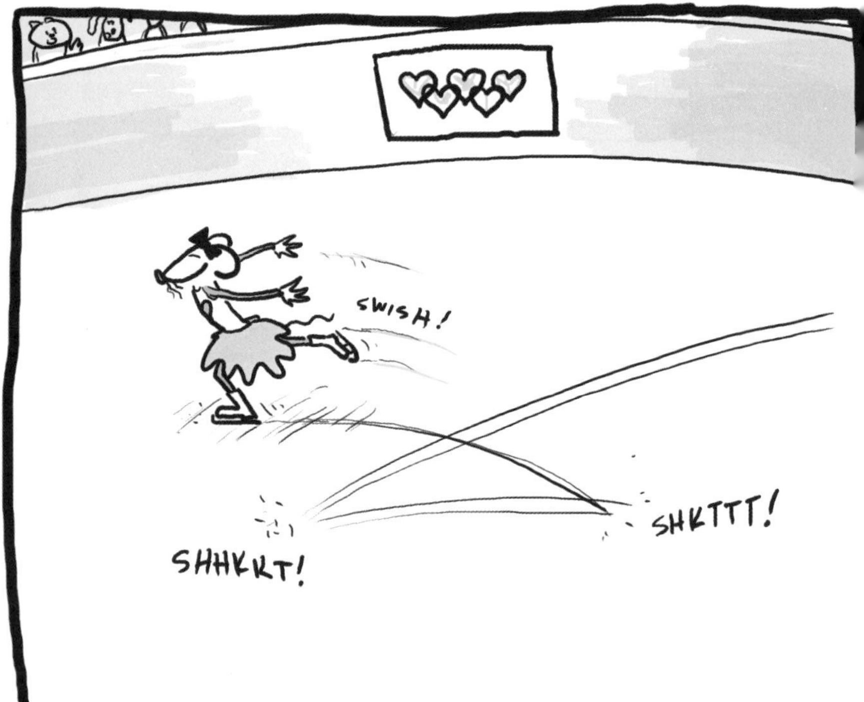
SWISH!
SHHKKT!
SHKTTT!

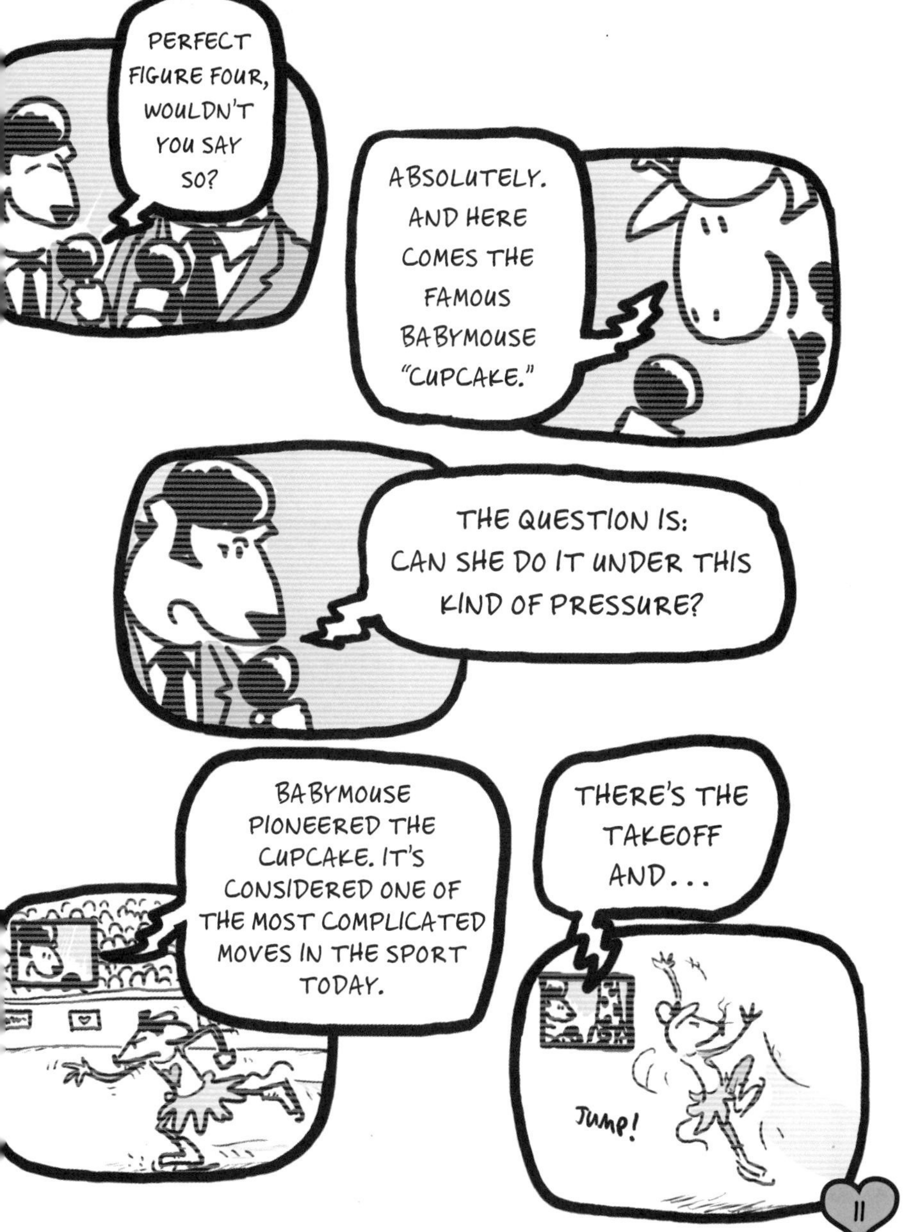
PERFECT FIGURE FOUR, WOULDN'T YOU SAY SO?
ABSOLUTELY. AND HERE COMES THE FAMOUS BABYMOUSE "CUPCAKE."
THE QUESTION IS: CAN SHE DO IT UNDER THIS KIND OF PRESSURE?
BABYMOUSE PIONEERED THE CUPCAKE. IT'S CONSIDERED ONE OF THE MOST COMPLICATED MOVES IN THE SPORT TODAY.
THERE'S THE TAKEOFF AND . . .
JUMP!

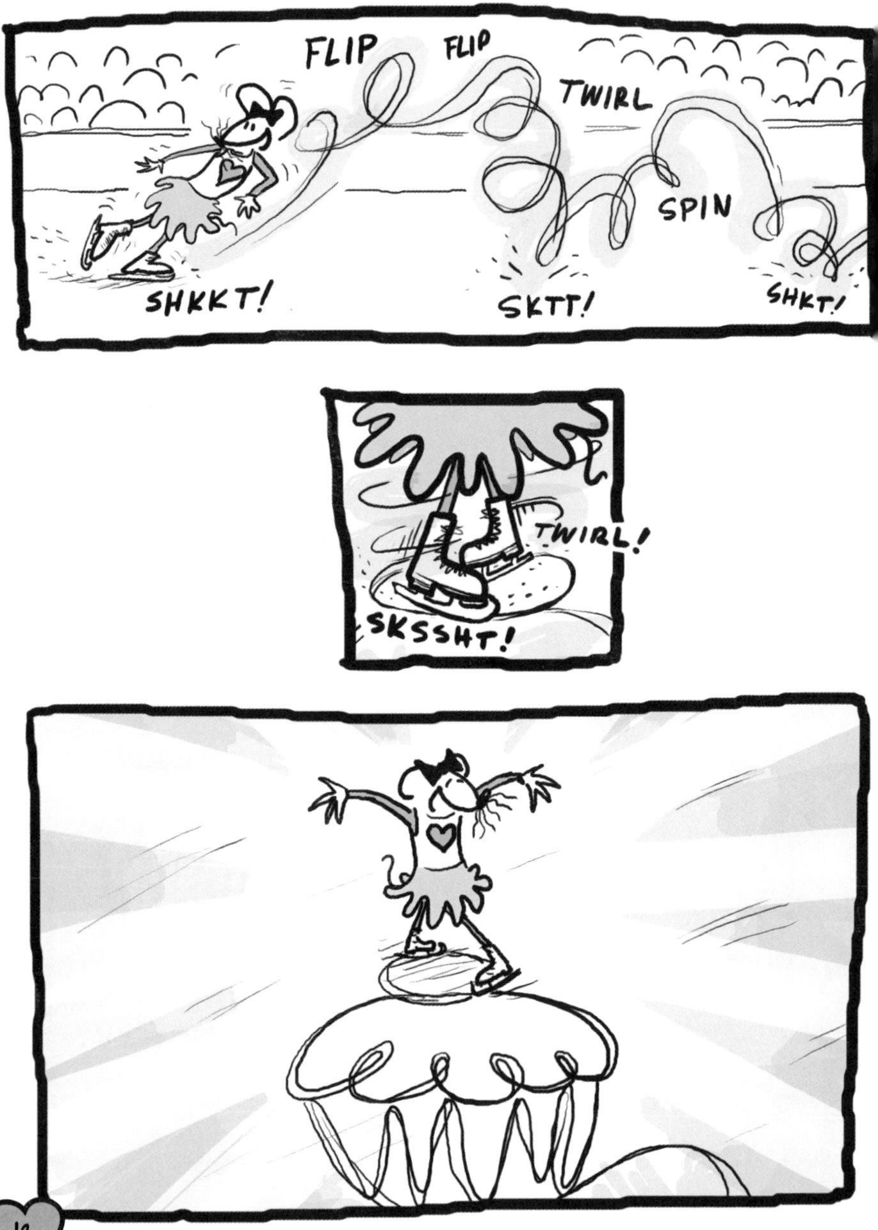
SHKKT!
FLIP
FLIP
TWIRL
SKTT!
SPIN
SHKT!
TWIRL!
SKSSHT!

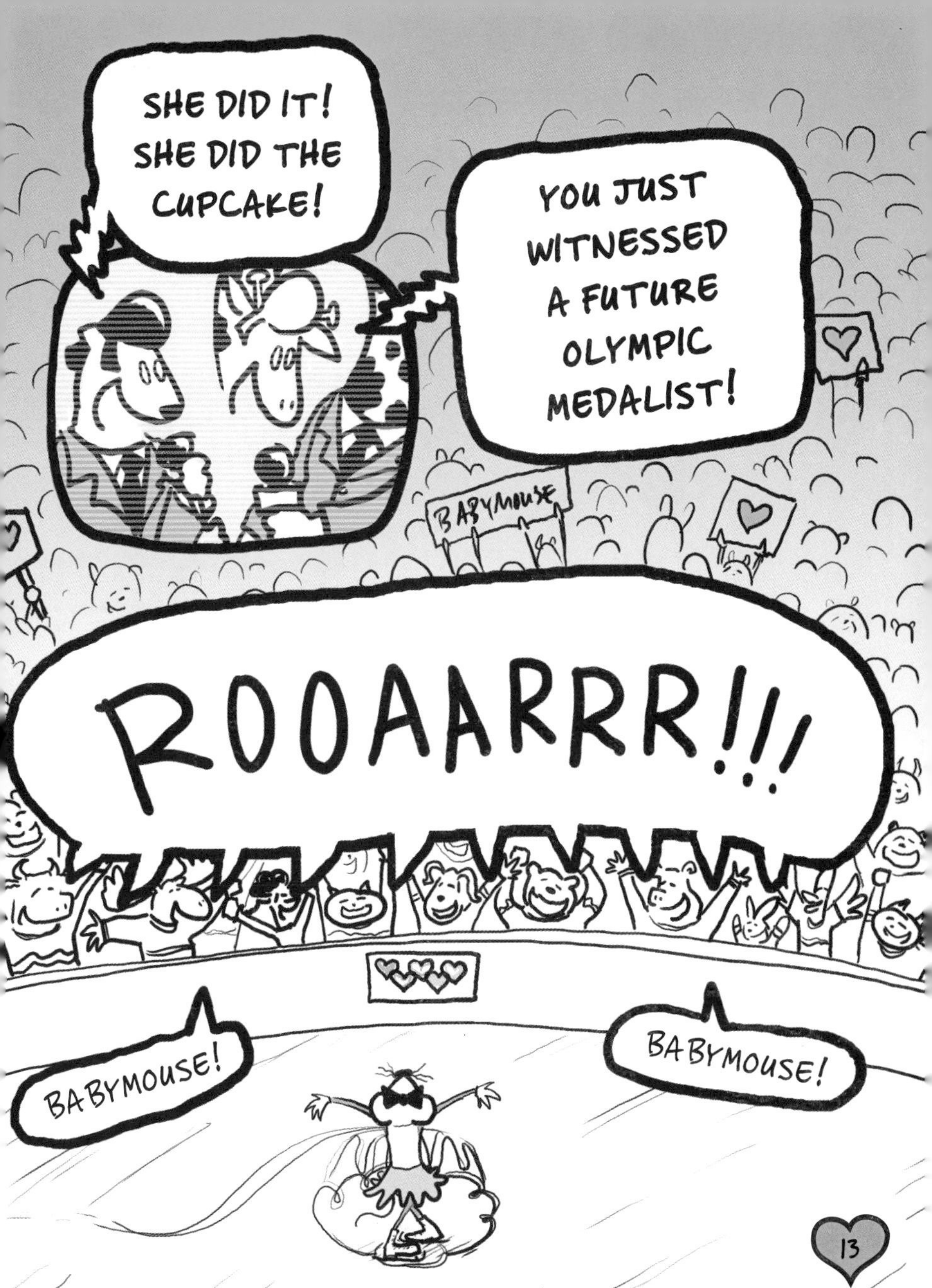
SHE DID IT! SHE DID THE CUPCAKE!
YOU JUST WITNESSED A FUTURE OLYMPIC MEDALIST!
BABYMOUSE
ROOAARRR!!!
BABYMOUSE!
BABYMOUSE!

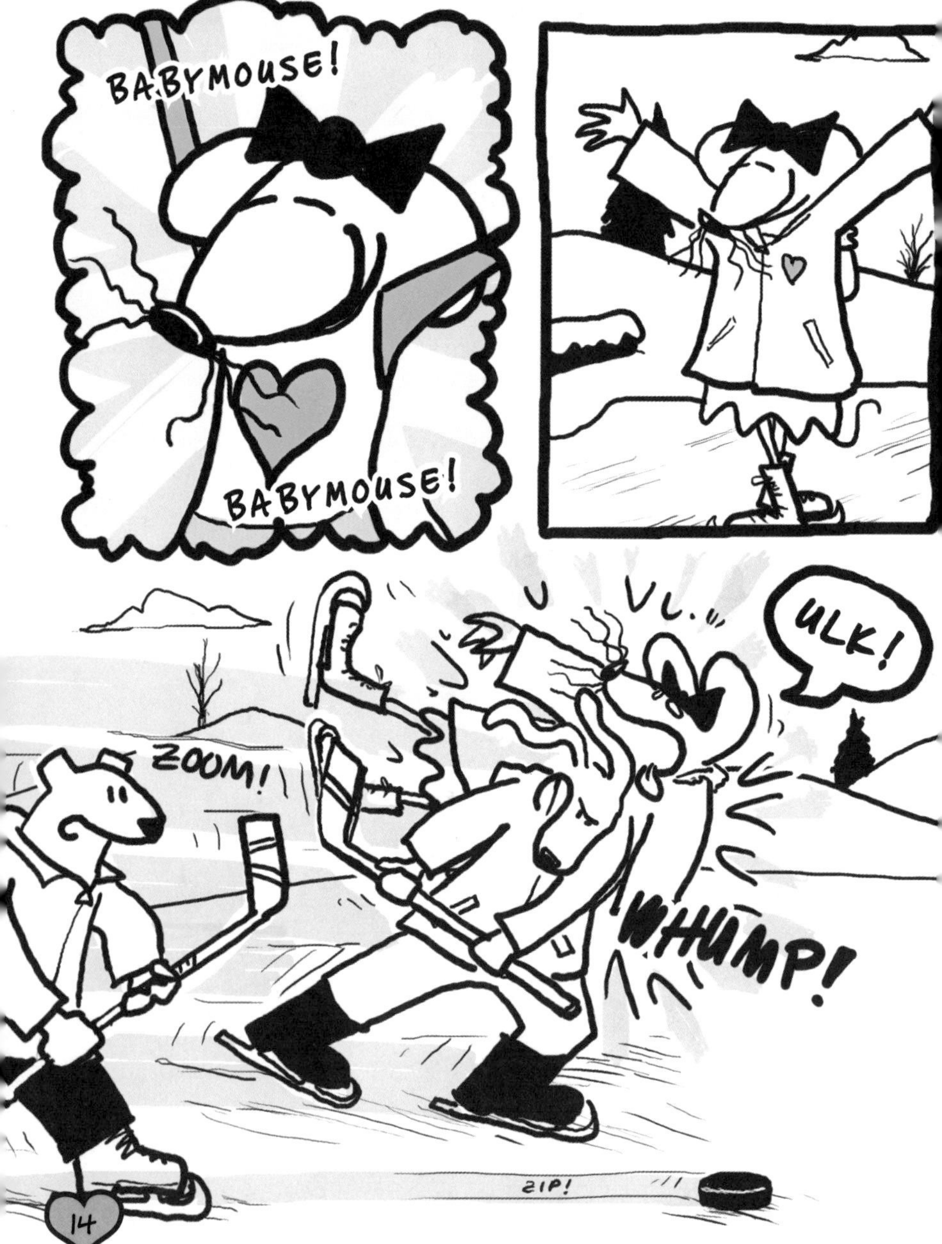
BABYMOUSE!
BABYMOUSE!
ZOOM!
ULK!
WHUMP!
ZIP!

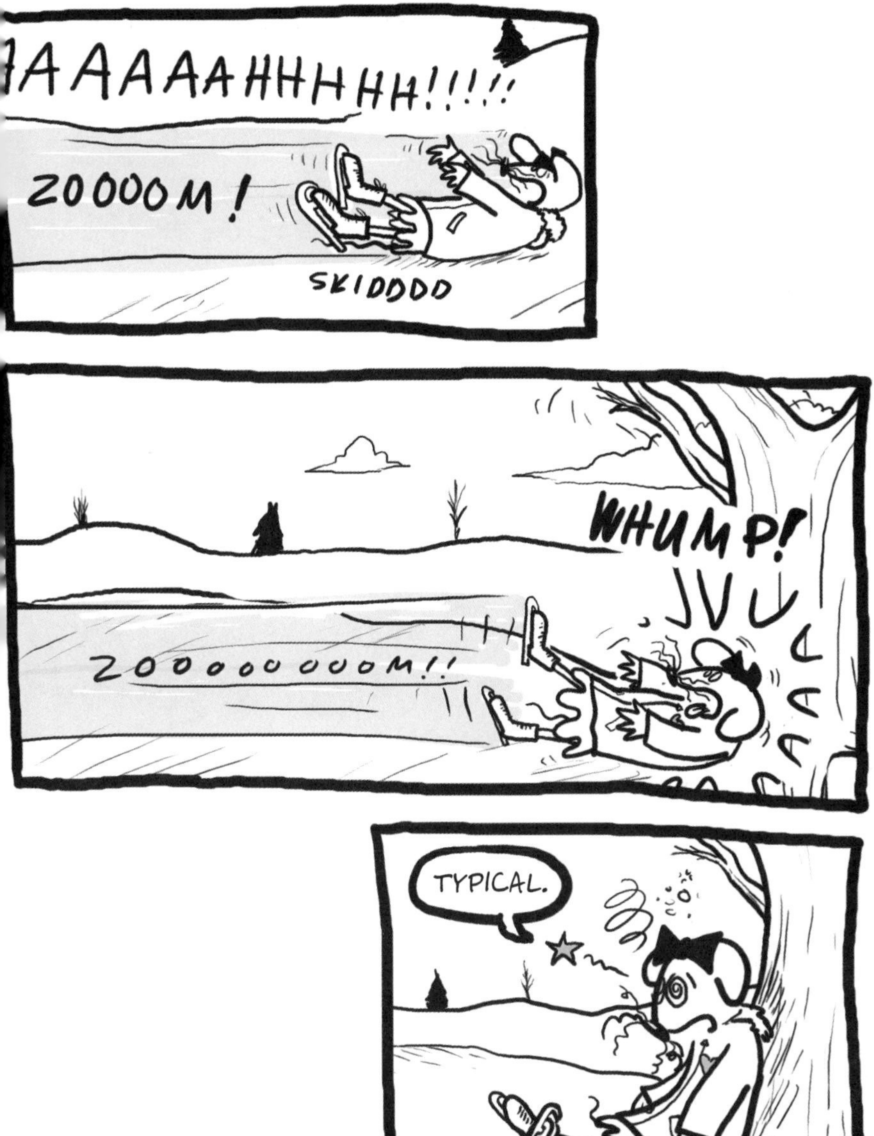
AAAAAAHHHHHH!!!!!
ZOOOOM!
SKIDDDD
WHUMP!
ZOOOOOOOOOM!!
TYPICAL.

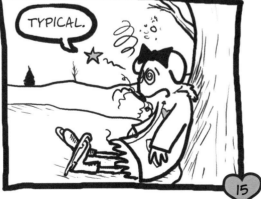

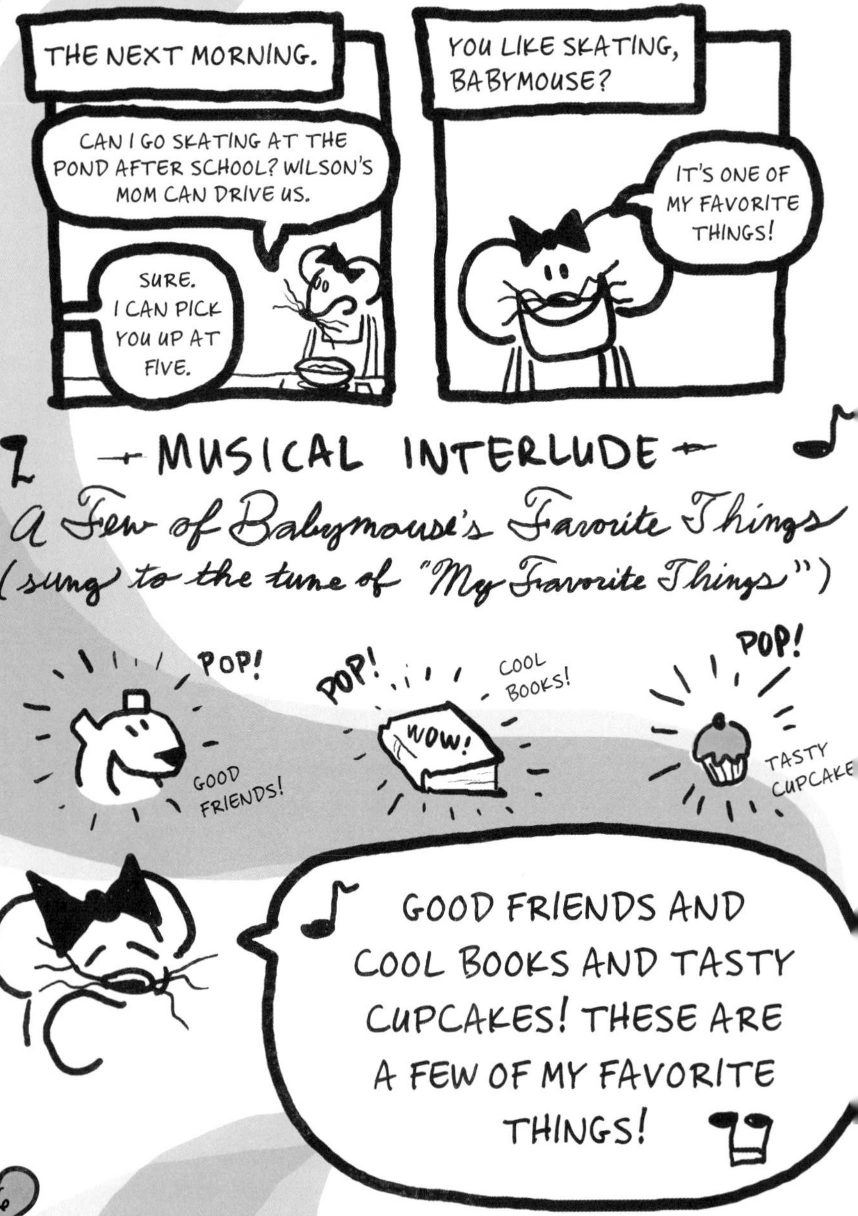
THE NEXT MORNING.
CAN I GO SKATING AT THE POND AFTER SCHOOL? WILSON'S MOM CAN DRIVE US.
SURE. I CAN PICK YOU UP AT FIVE.
YOU LIKE SKATING, BABYMOUSE?
IT'S ONE OF MY FAVORITE THINGS!
MUSICAL INTERLUDE
A Few of Babymouse's Favorite Things
(sung to the tune of "My Favorite Things")
POP!
GOOD FRIENDS!
POP!
WOW!
COOL BOOKS!
POP!
TASTY CUPCAKE
GOOD FRIENDS AND COOL BOOKS AND TASTY CUPCAKES! THESE ARE A FEW OF MY FAVORITE THINGS!

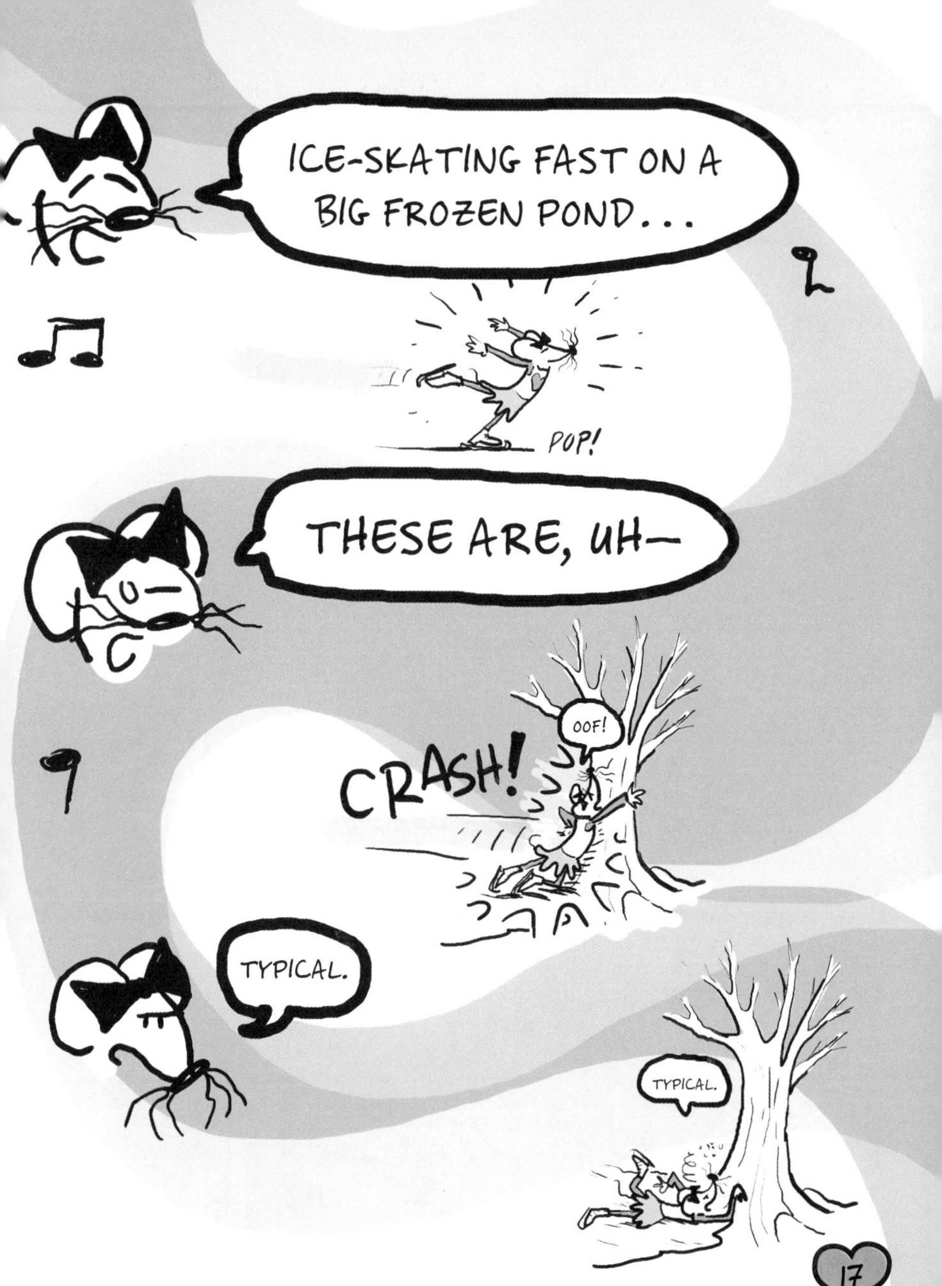
ICE-SKATING FAST ON A BIG FROZEN POND...
POP!
THESE ARE, UH—
OOF!
CRASH!
TYPICAL.
TYPICAL.

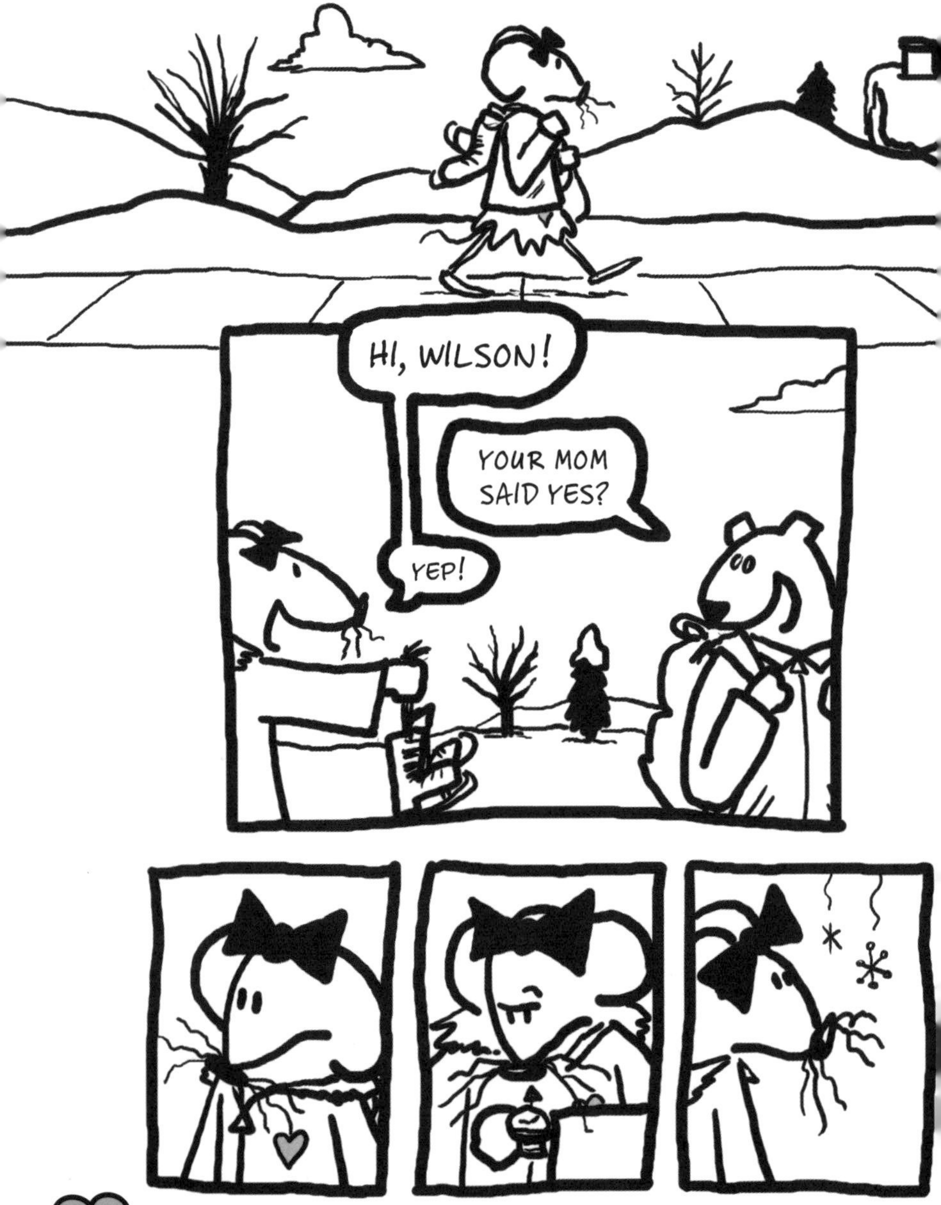
HI, WILSON!
YOUR MOM SAID YES?
YEP!

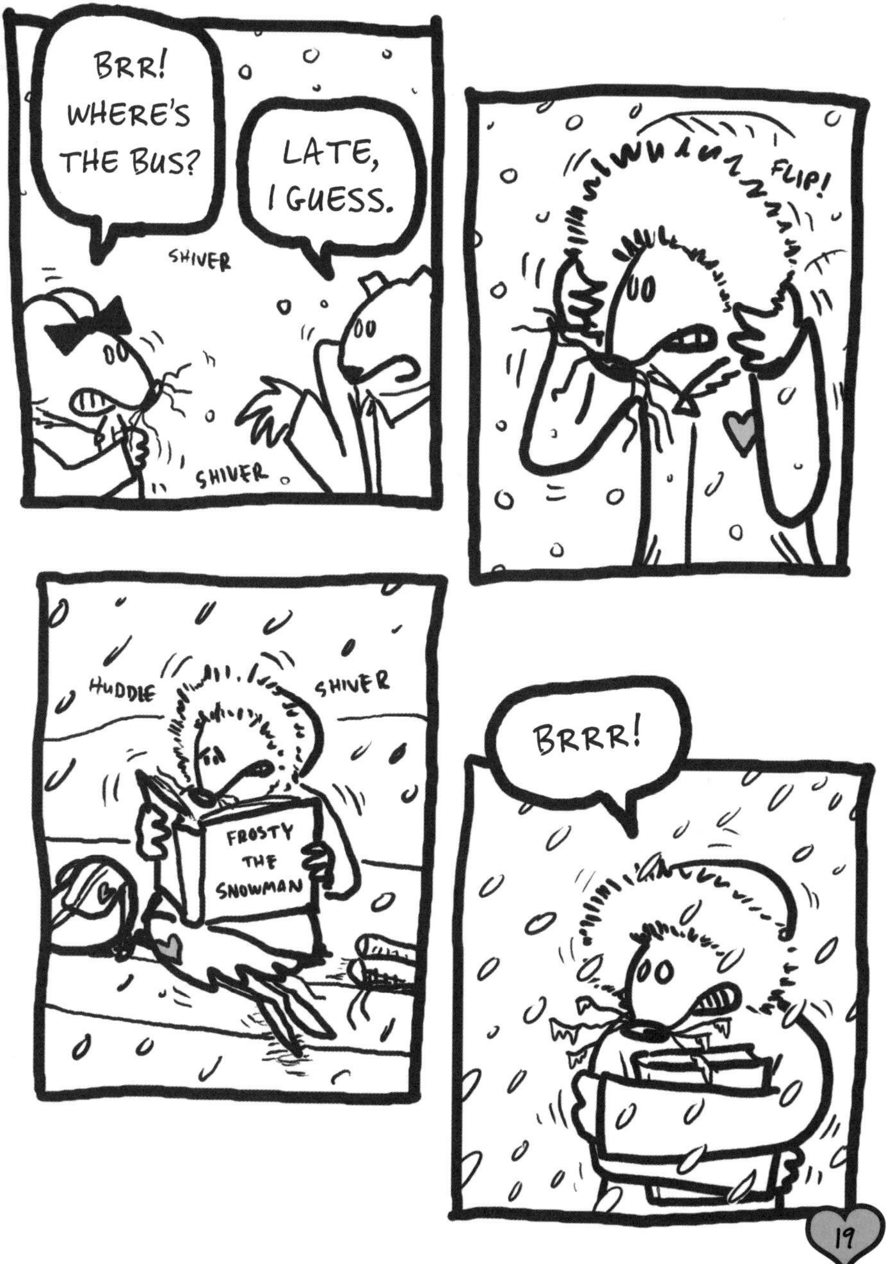
BRR! WHERE'S THE BUS?
LATE, I GUESS.
SHIVER
SHIVER
FLIP!
HUDDLE
SHIVER
FROSTY THE SNOWMAN
BRRR!

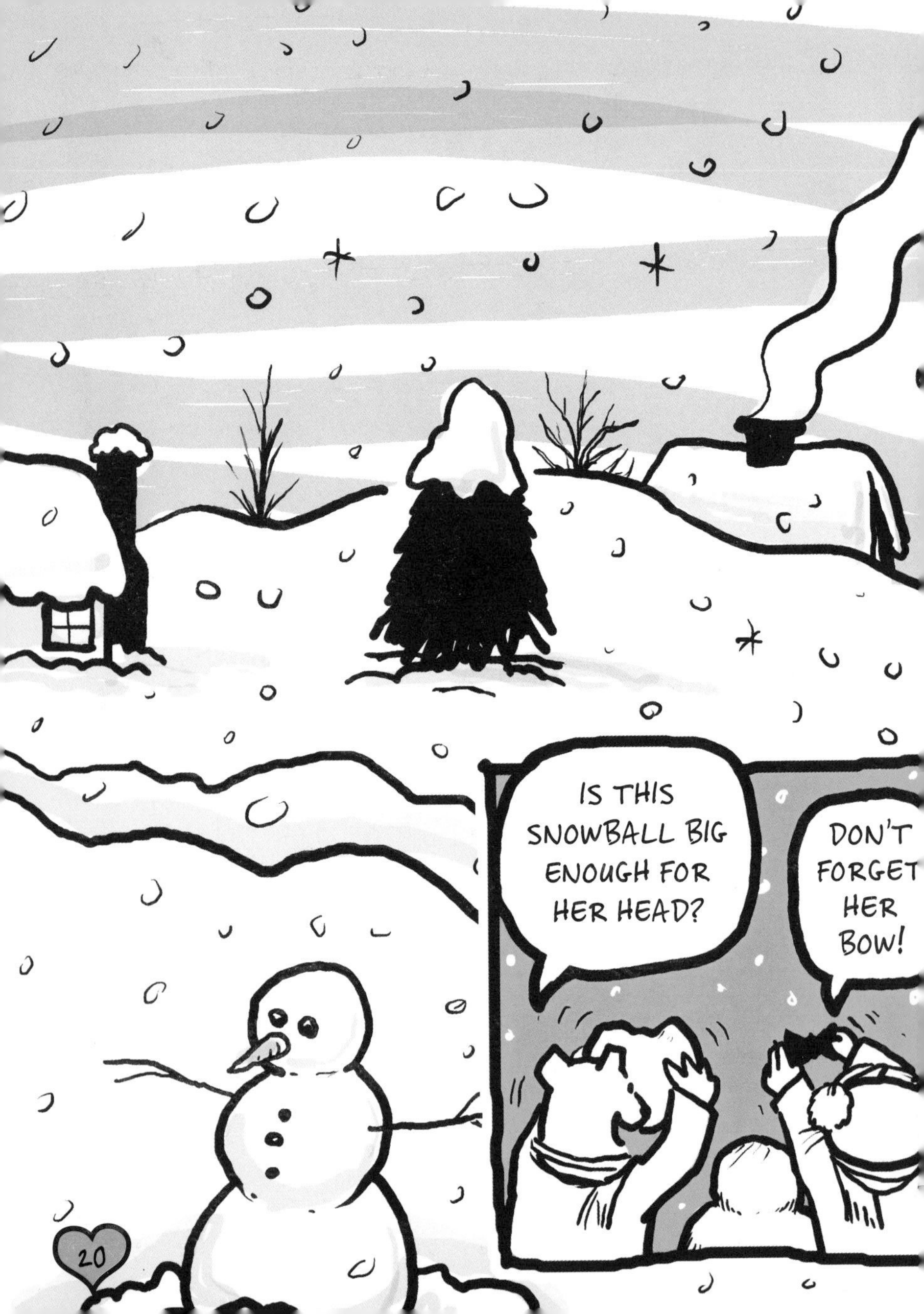
IS THIS SNOWBALL BIG ENOUGH FOR HER HEAD?
DON'T FORGET HER BOW!

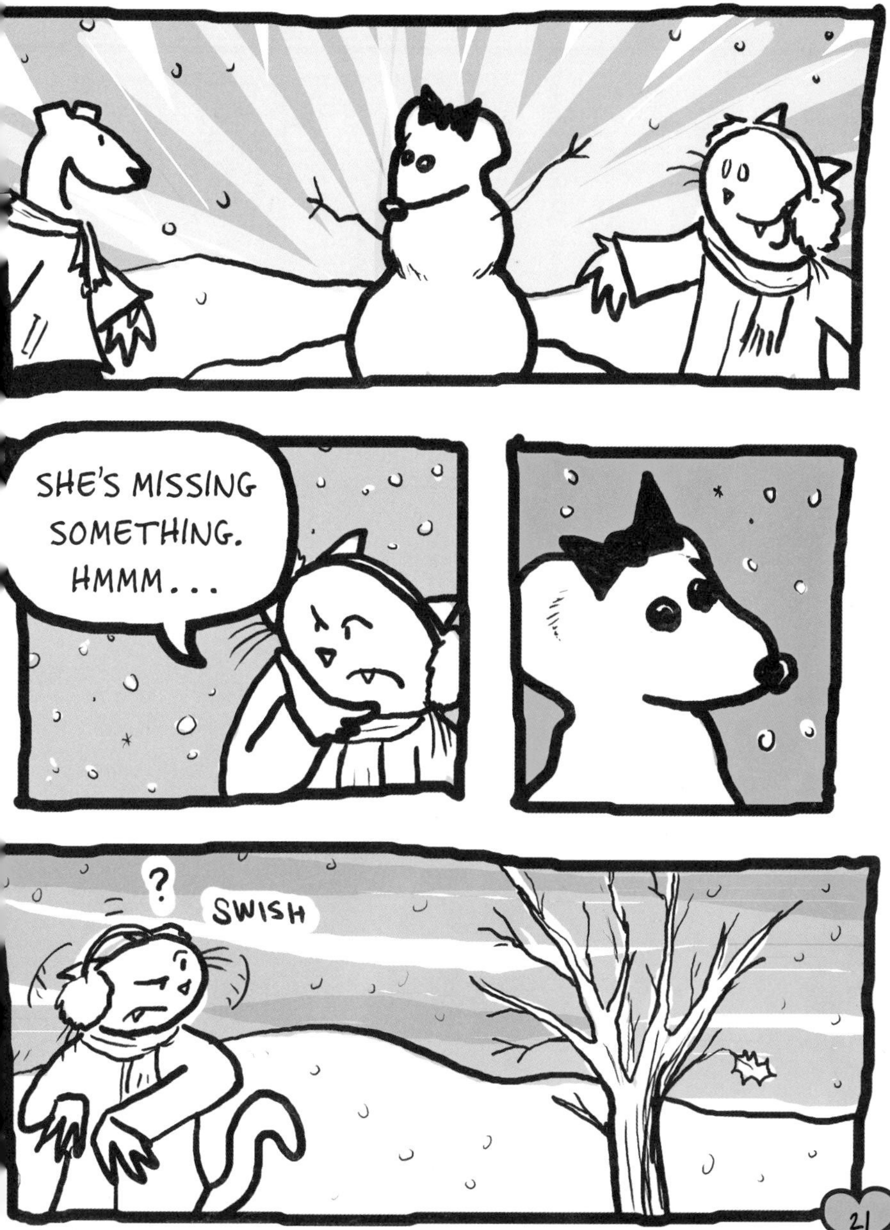
SHE'S MISSING SOMETHING. HMMM...
?
SWISH

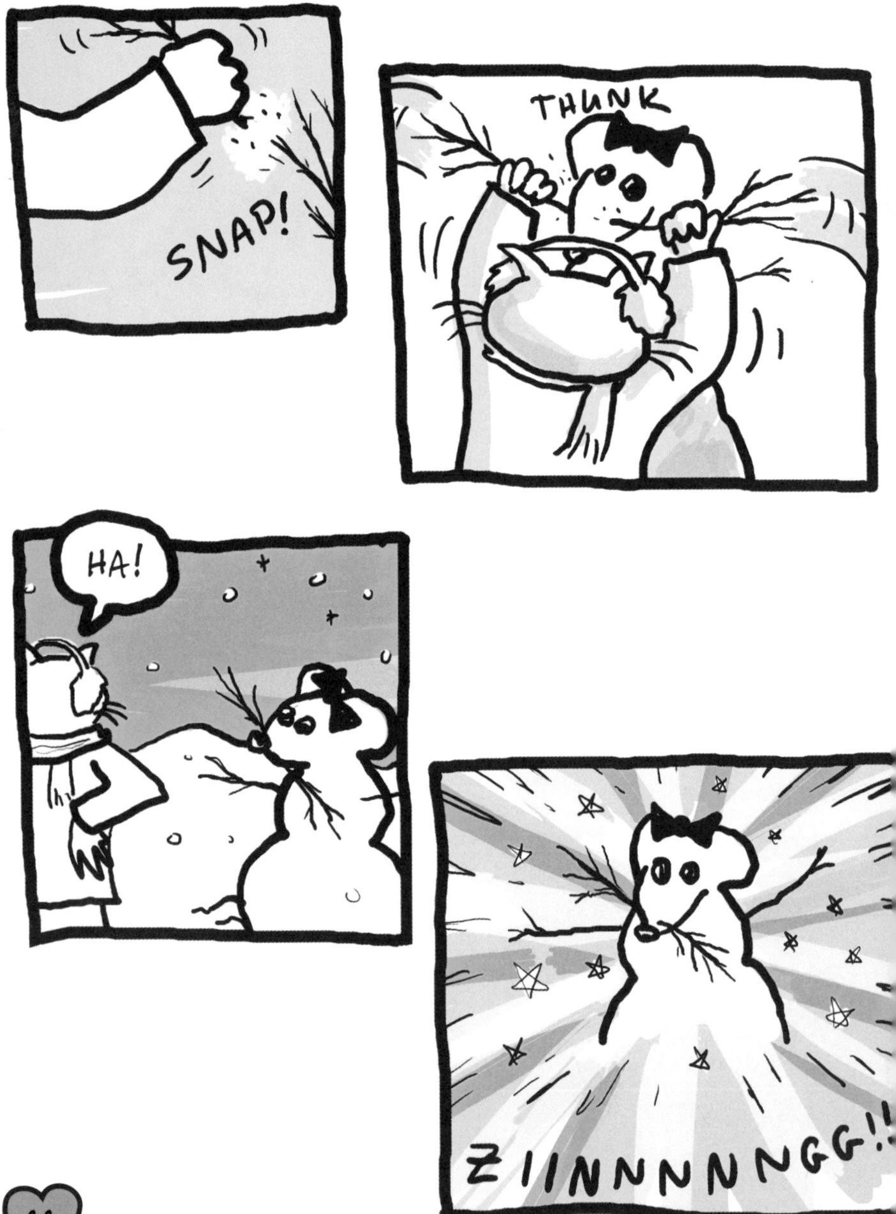
SNAP!
THUNK
HA!
ZIINNNNNGG!!

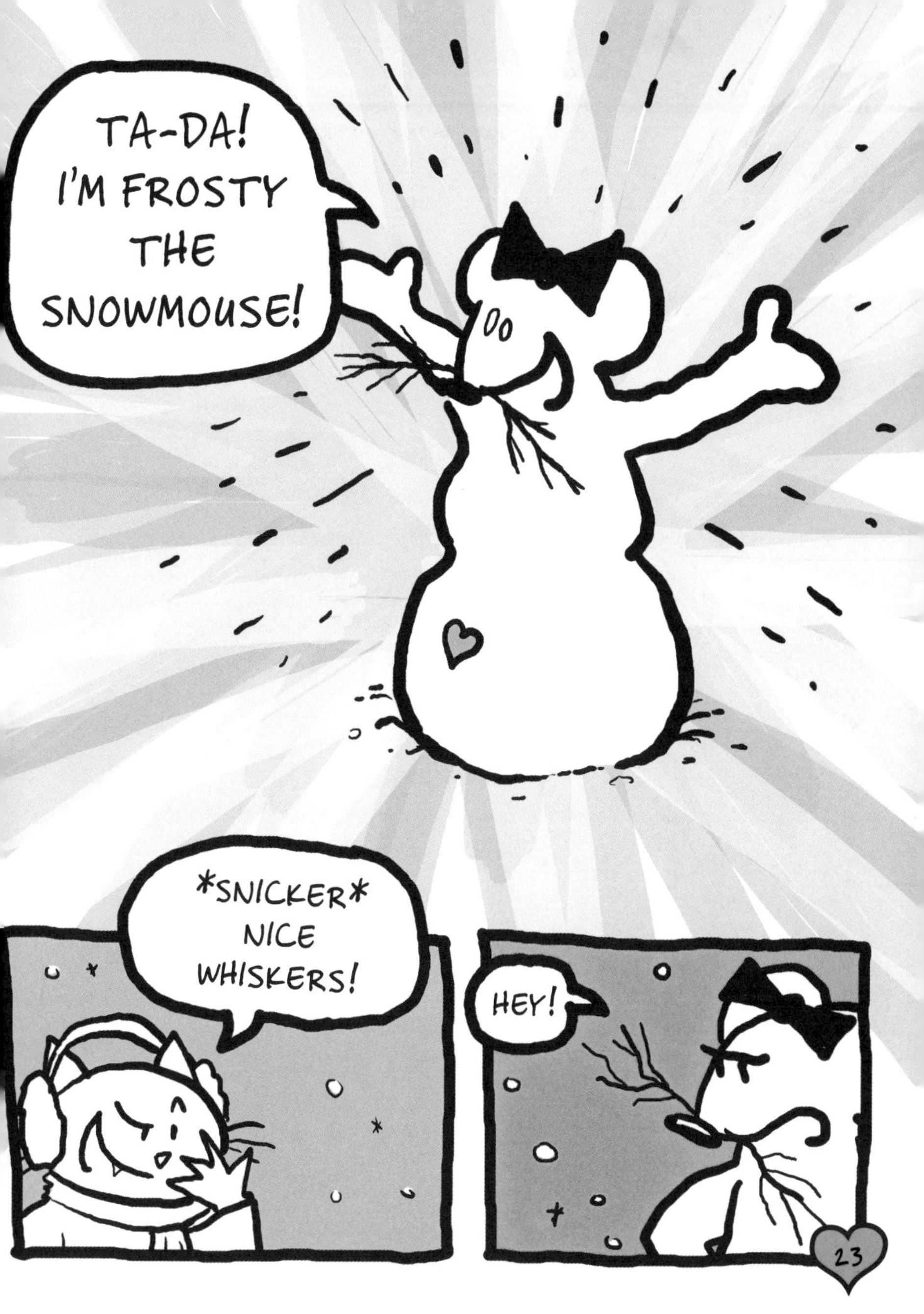
TA-DA! I'M FROSTY THE SNOWMOUSE!
SNICKER NICE WHISKERS!
HEY!

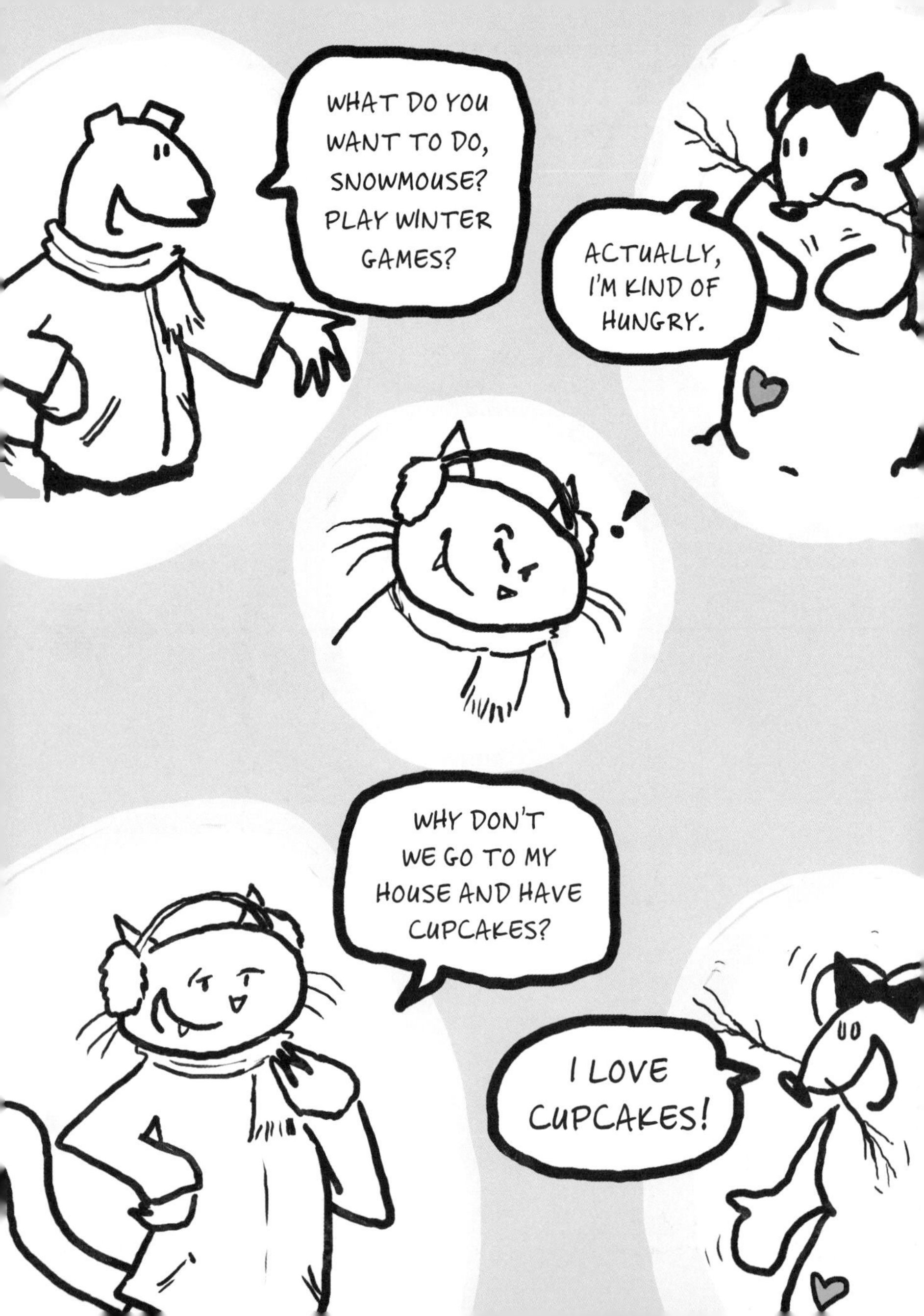
WHAT DO YOU WANT TO DO, SNOWMOUSE? PLAY WINTER GAMES?
ACTUALLY, I'M KIND OF HUNGRY.
!
WHY DON'T WE GO TO MY HOUSE AND HAVE CUPCAKES?
I LOVE CUPCAKES!

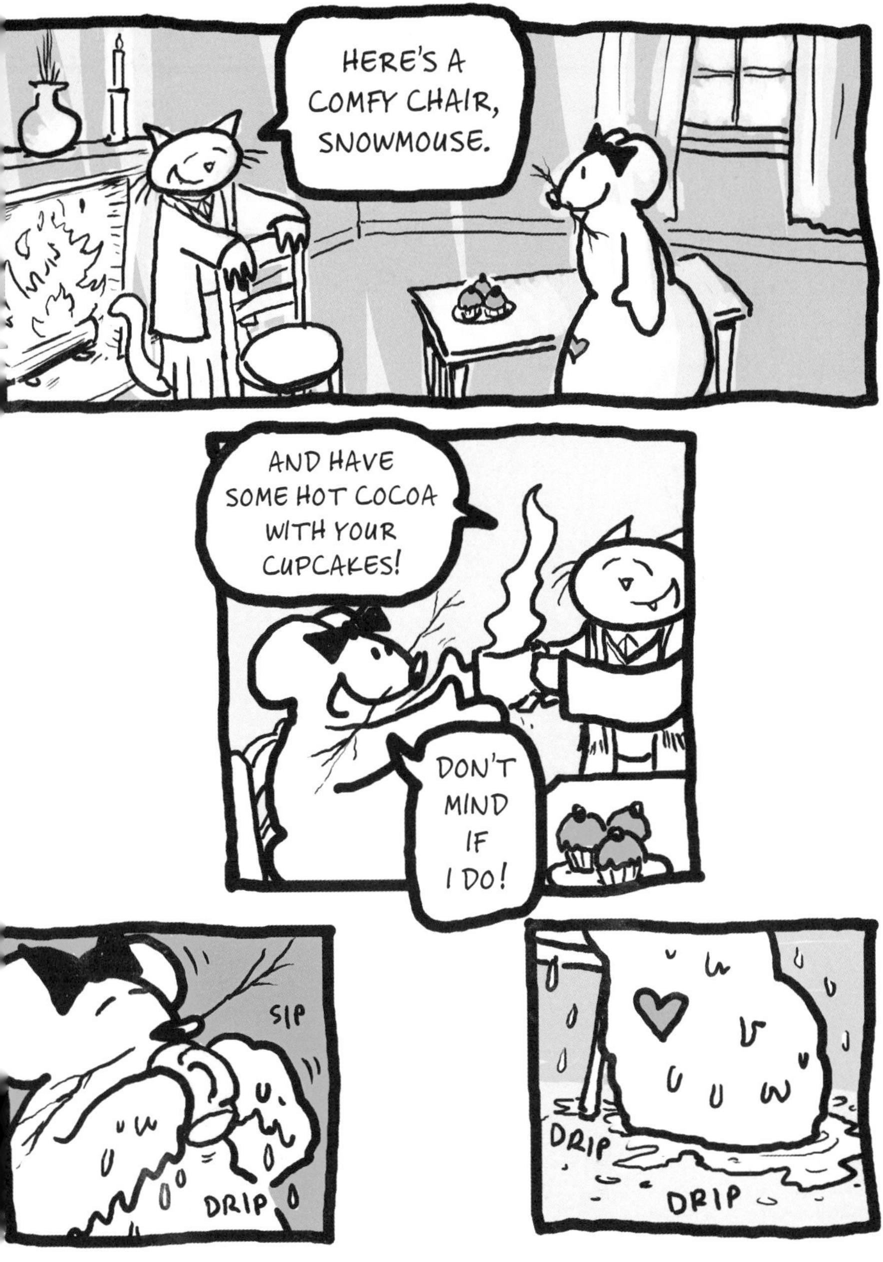
HERE'S A COMFY CHAIR, SNOWMOUSE.
AND HAVE SOME HOT COCOA WITH YOUR CUPCAKES!
DON'T MIND IF I DO!
SIP
DRIP
DRIP
DRIP

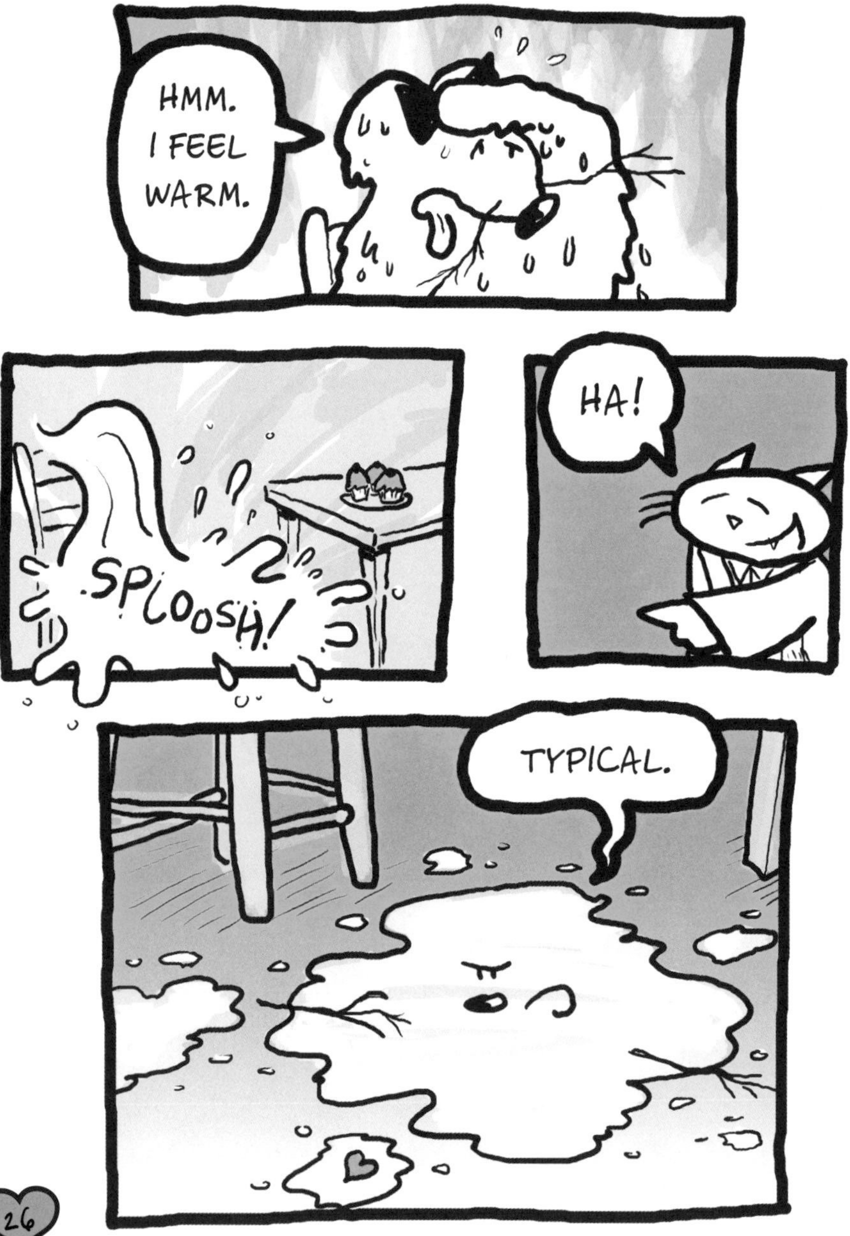
HMM. I FEEL WARM.
SPLOOSH!
HA!
TYPICAL.

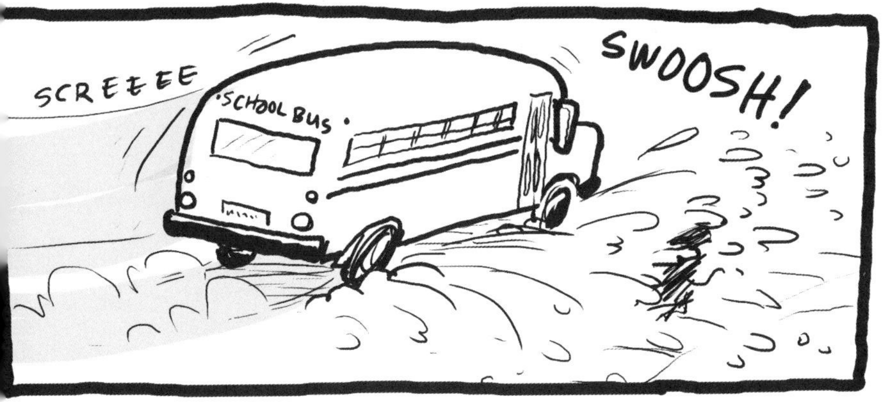
SCREEEE
SCHOOL BUS
SWOOSH!

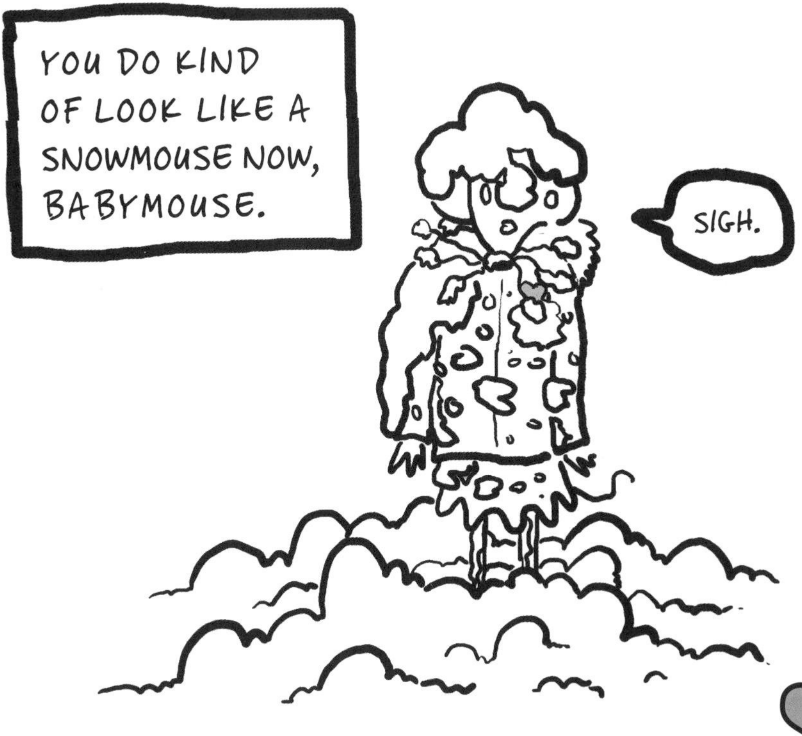
YOU DO KIND OF LOOK LIKE A SNOWMOUSE NOW, BABYMOUSE.
SIGH.

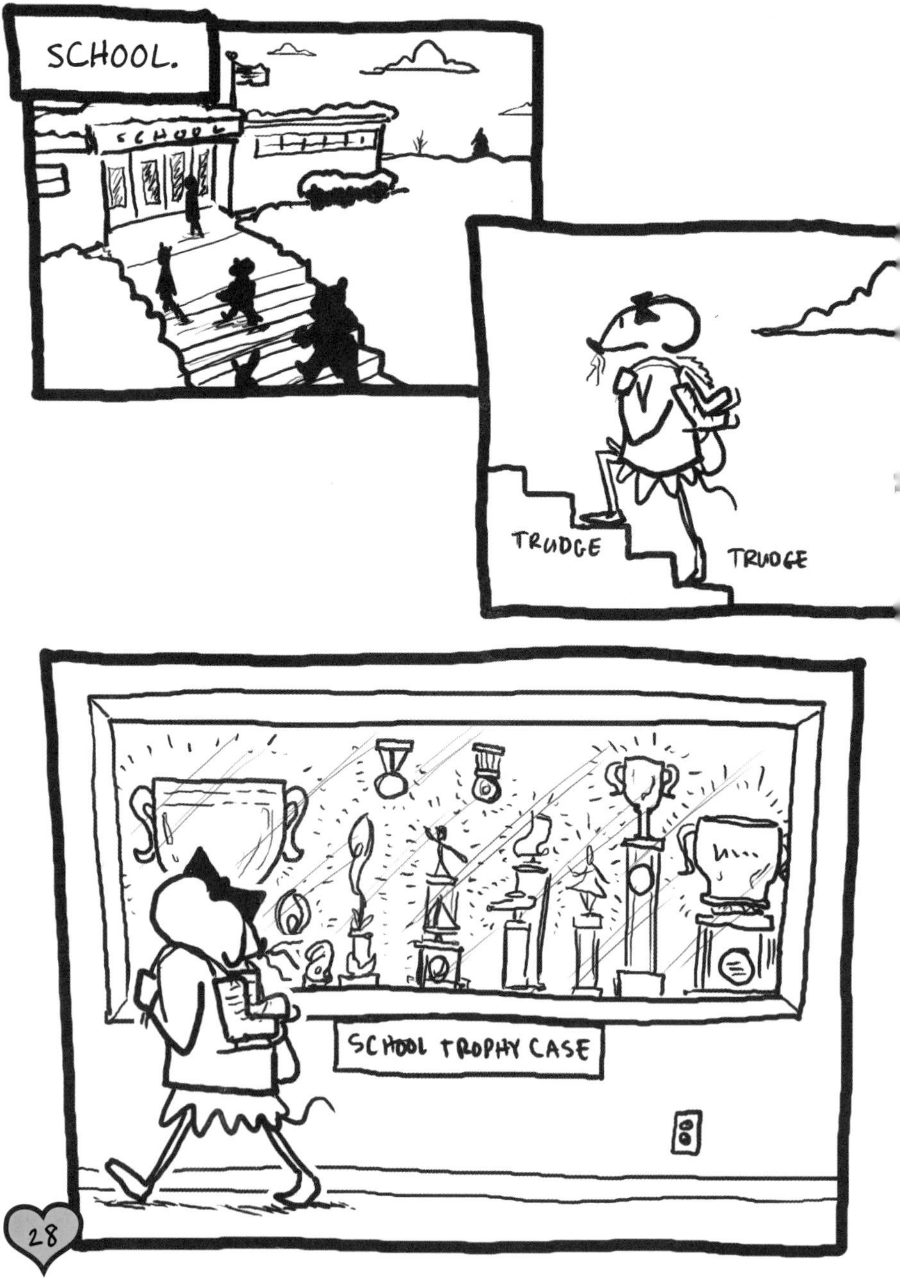
SCHOOL.
TRUDGE
TRUDGE
SCHOOL TROPHY CASE

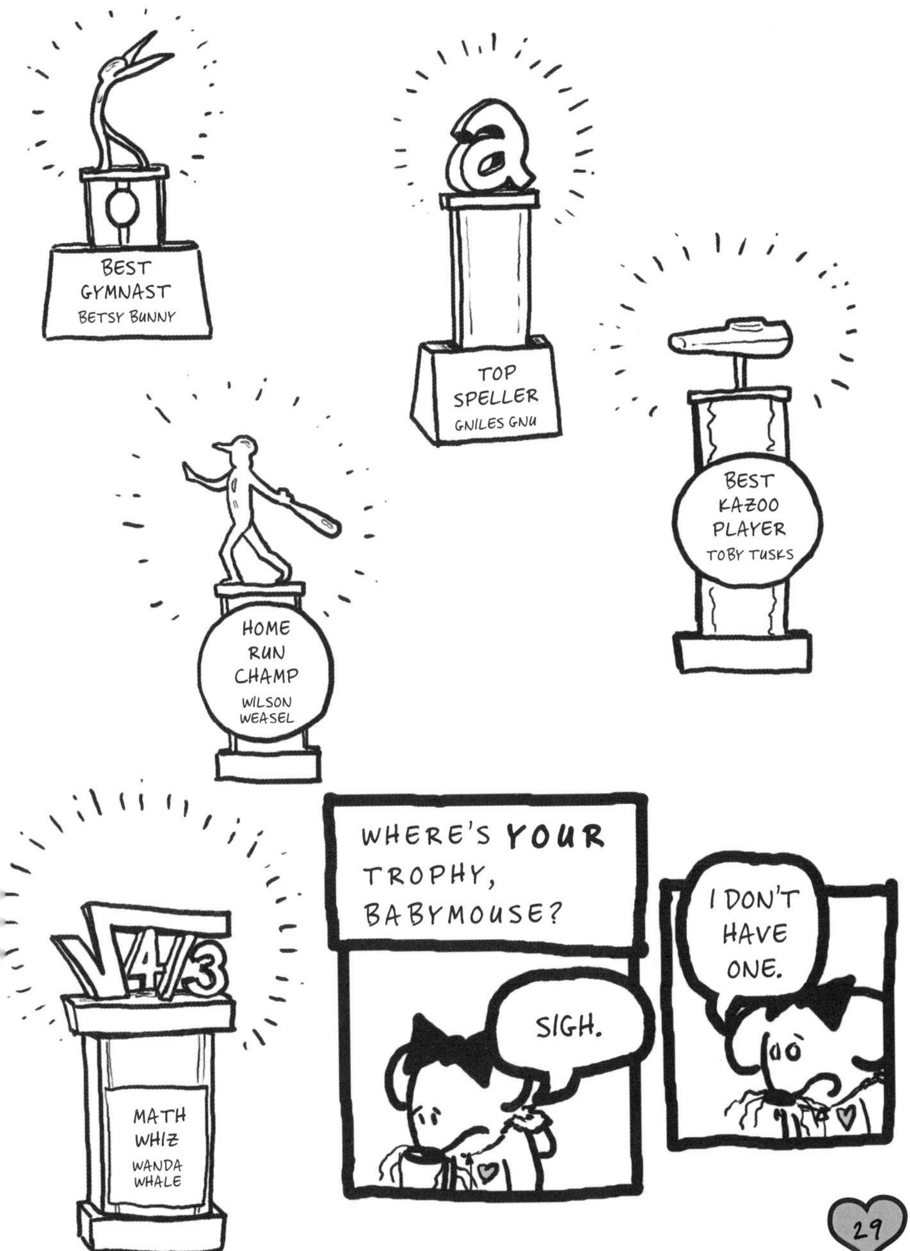
BEST GYMNAST
BETSY BUNNY
TOP SPELLER
GNILES GNU
BEST KAZOO PLAYER
TOBY TUSKS
HOME RUN CHAMP
WILSON WEASEL
MATH WHIZ
WANDA WHALE
WHERE'S **YOUR** TROPHY, BABYMOUSE?
SIGH.
I DON'T HAVE ONE.

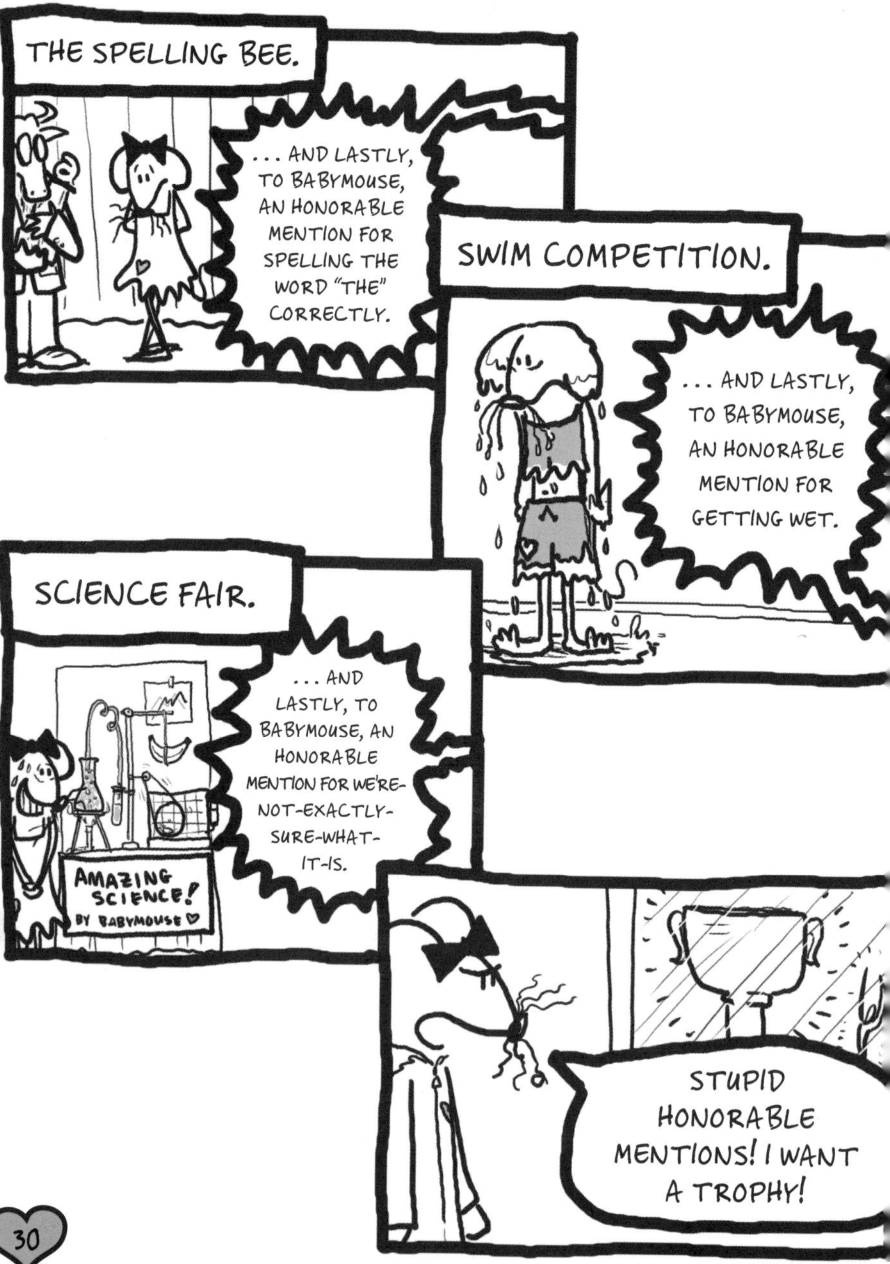
THE SPELLING BEE.
. . . AND LASTLY, TO BABYMOUSE, AN HONORABLE MENTION FOR SPELLING THE WORD "THE" CORRECTLY.
SWIM COMPETITION.
. . . AND LASTLY, TO BABYMOUSE, AN HONORABLE MENTION FOR GETTING WET.
SCIENCE FAIR.
AMAZING SCIENCE! BY BABYMOUSE
. . . AND LASTLY, TO BABYMOUSE, AN HONORABLE MENTION FOR WE'RE-NOT-EXACTLY-SURE-WHAT-IT-IS.
STUPID HONORABLE MENTIONS! I WANT A TROPHY!

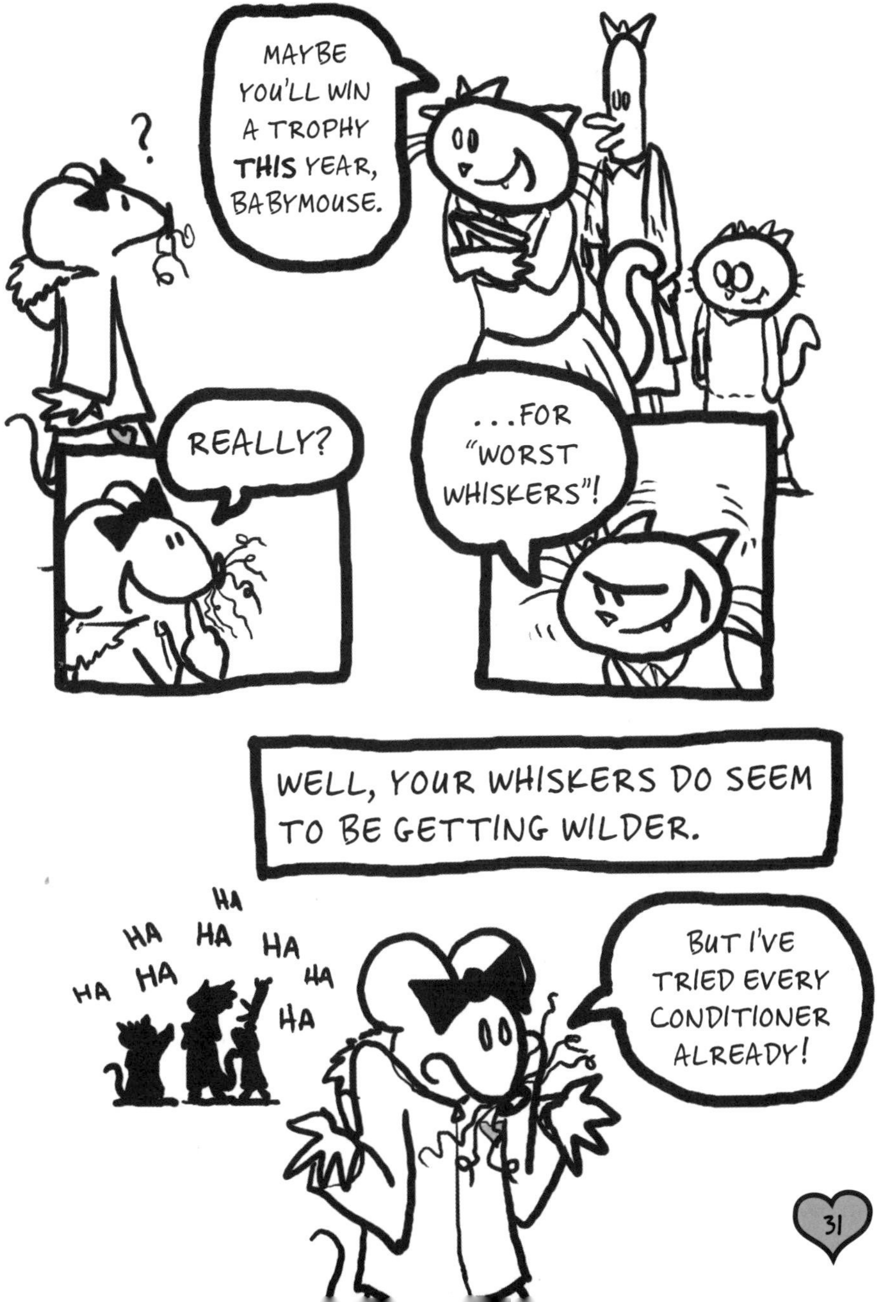
MAYBE YOU'LL WIN A TROPHY **THIS** YEAR, BABYMOUSE.
?
REALLY?
...FOR "WORST WHISKERS"!
WELL, YOUR WHISKERS DO SEEM TO BE GETTING WILDER.
HA HA HA HA HA HA HA HA
BUT I'VE TRIED EVERY CONDITIONER ALREADY!

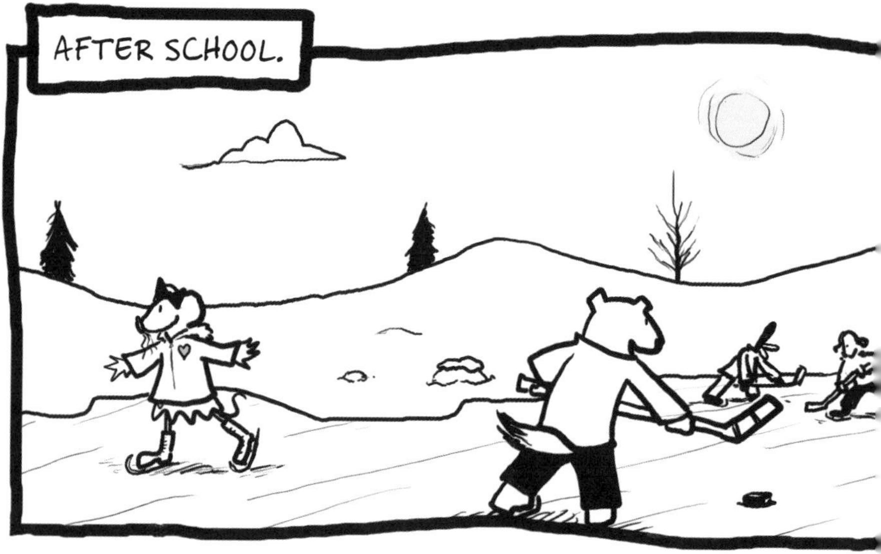
AFTER SCHOOL.

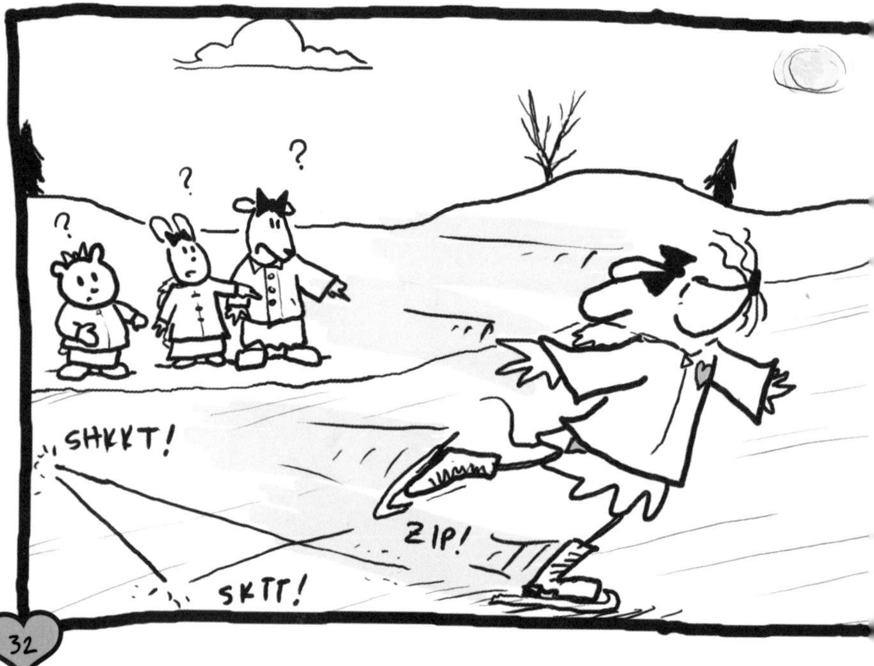
?
?
?
SHKKT!
ZIP!
SKTT!

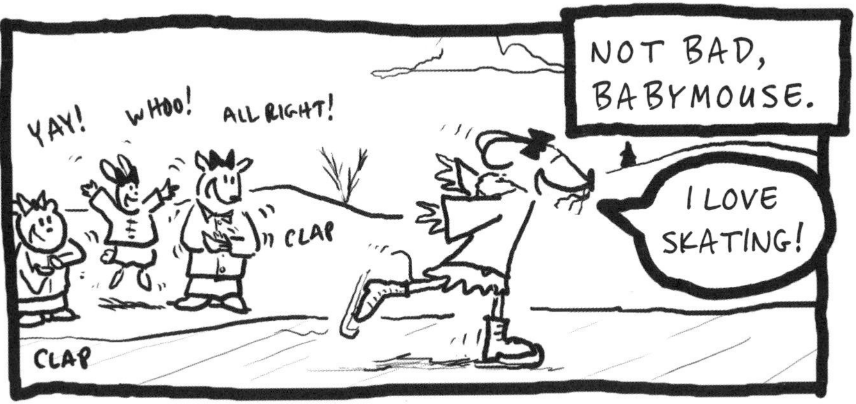
NOT BAD, BABYMOUSE.
YAY!
WHOO!
ALL RIGHT!
CLAP
CLAP
I LOVE SKATING!

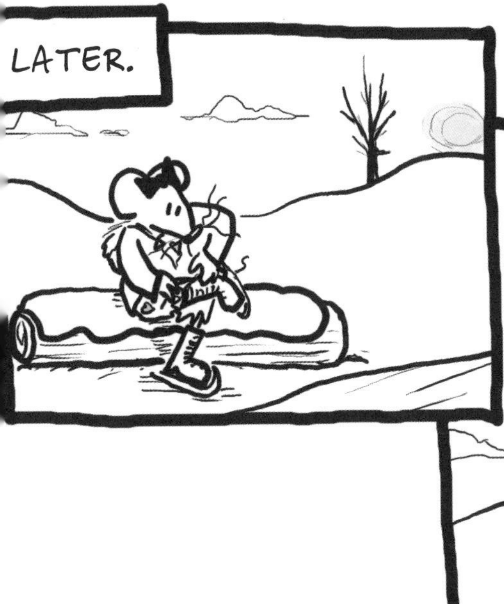
LATER.

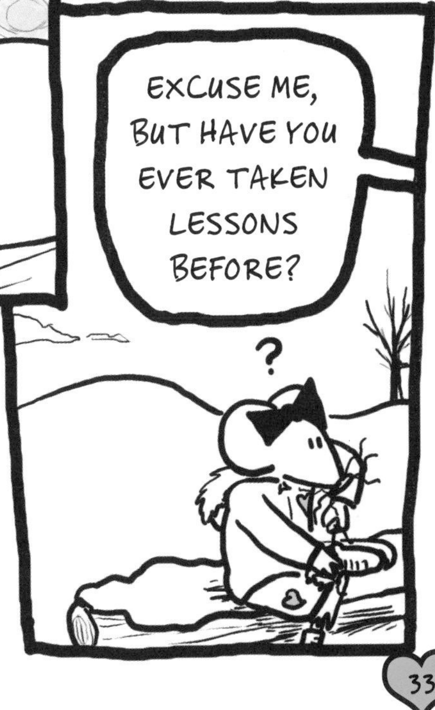
EXCUSE ME, BUT HAVE YOU EVER TAKEN LESSONS BEFORE?
?

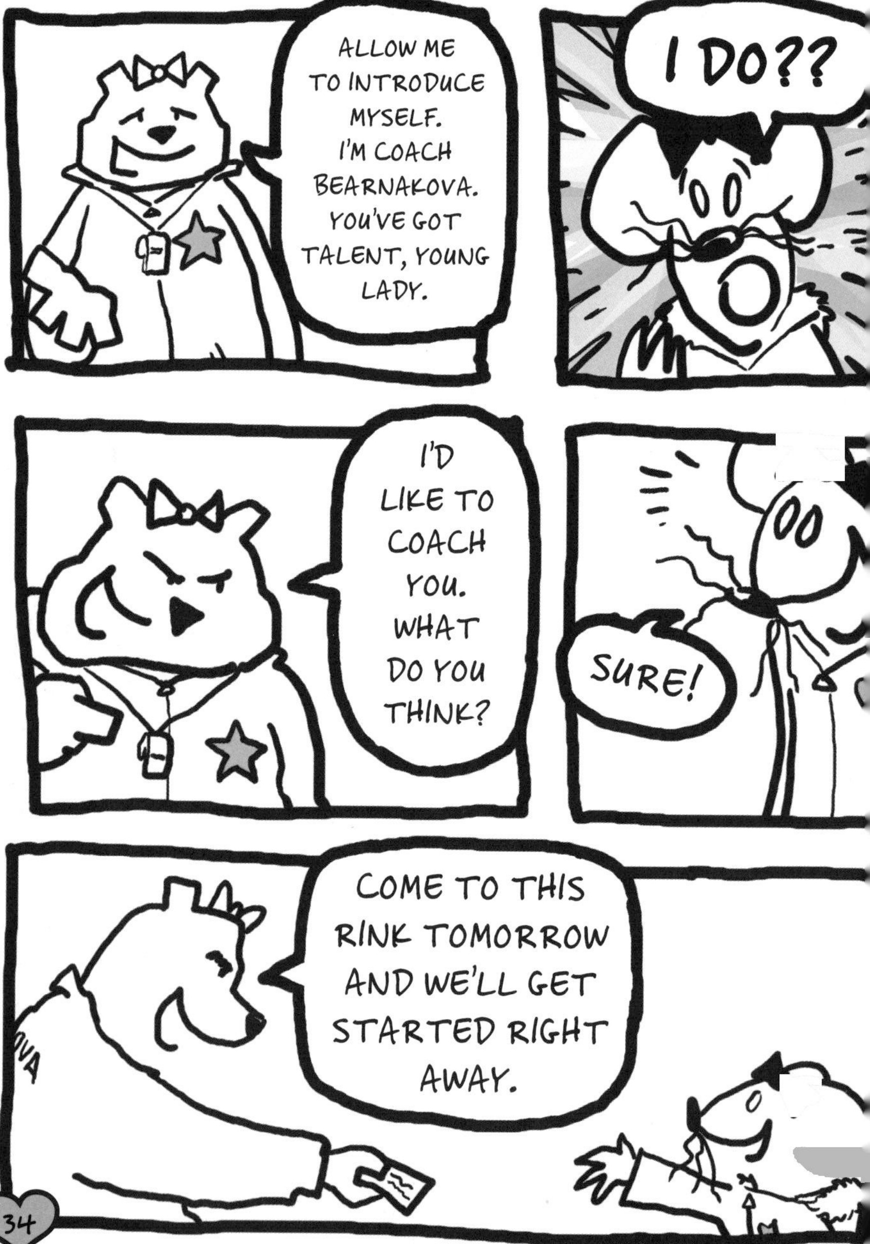
ALLOW ME TO INTRODUCE MYSELF. I'M COACH BEARNAKOVA. YOU'VE GOT TALENT, YOUNG LADY.
I DO??
I'D LIKE TO COACH YOU. WHAT DO YOU THINK?
SURE!
COME TO THIS RINK TOMORROW AND WE'LL GET STARTED RIGHT AWAY.

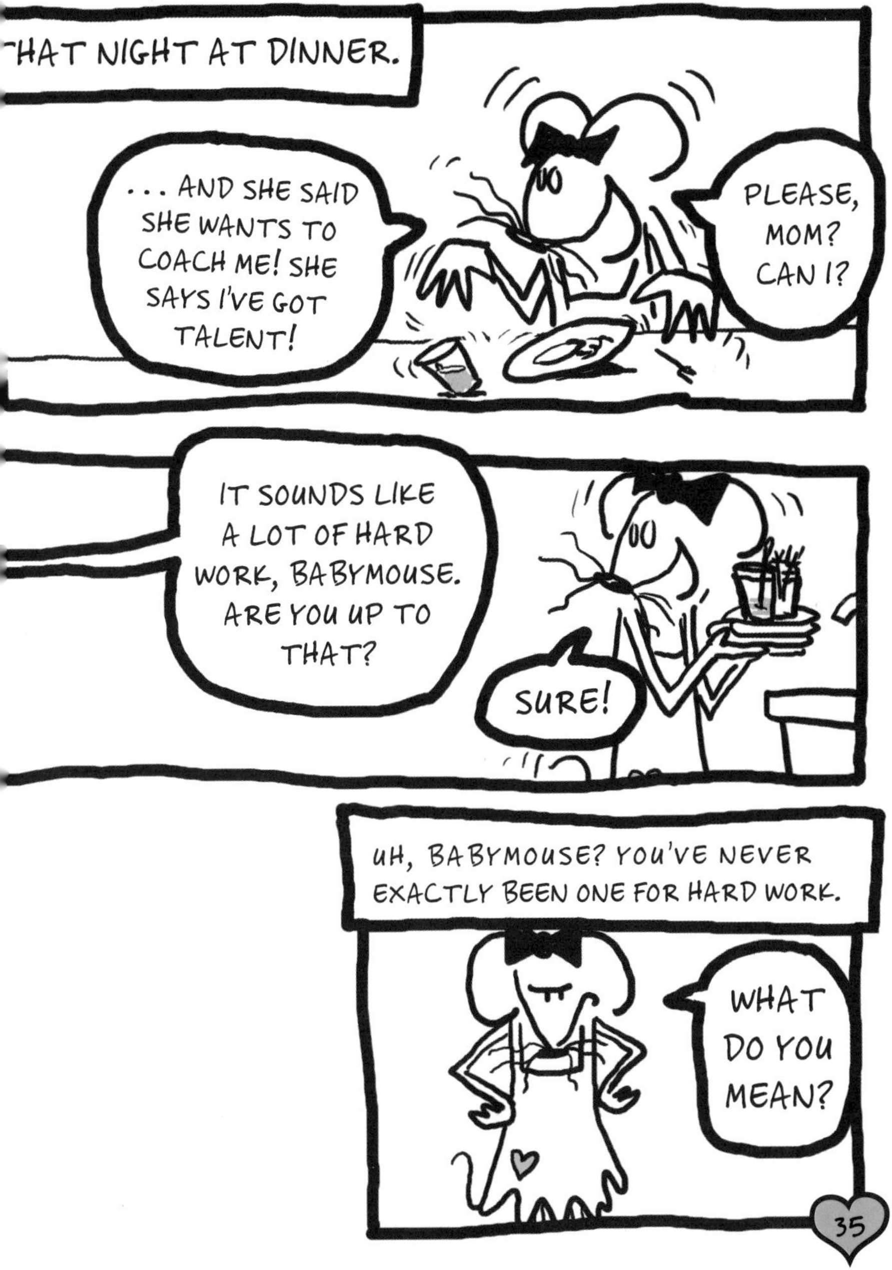
THAT NIGHT AT DINNER.
. . . AND SHE SAID SHE WANTS TO COACH ME! SHE SAYS I'VE GOT TALENT!
PLEASE, MOM? CAN I?
IT SOUNDS LIKE A LOT OF HARD WORK, BABYMOUSE. ARE YOU UP TO THAT?
SURE!
UH, BABYMOUSE? YOU'VE NEVER EXACTLY BEEN ONE FOR HARD WORK.
WHAT DO YOU MEAN?

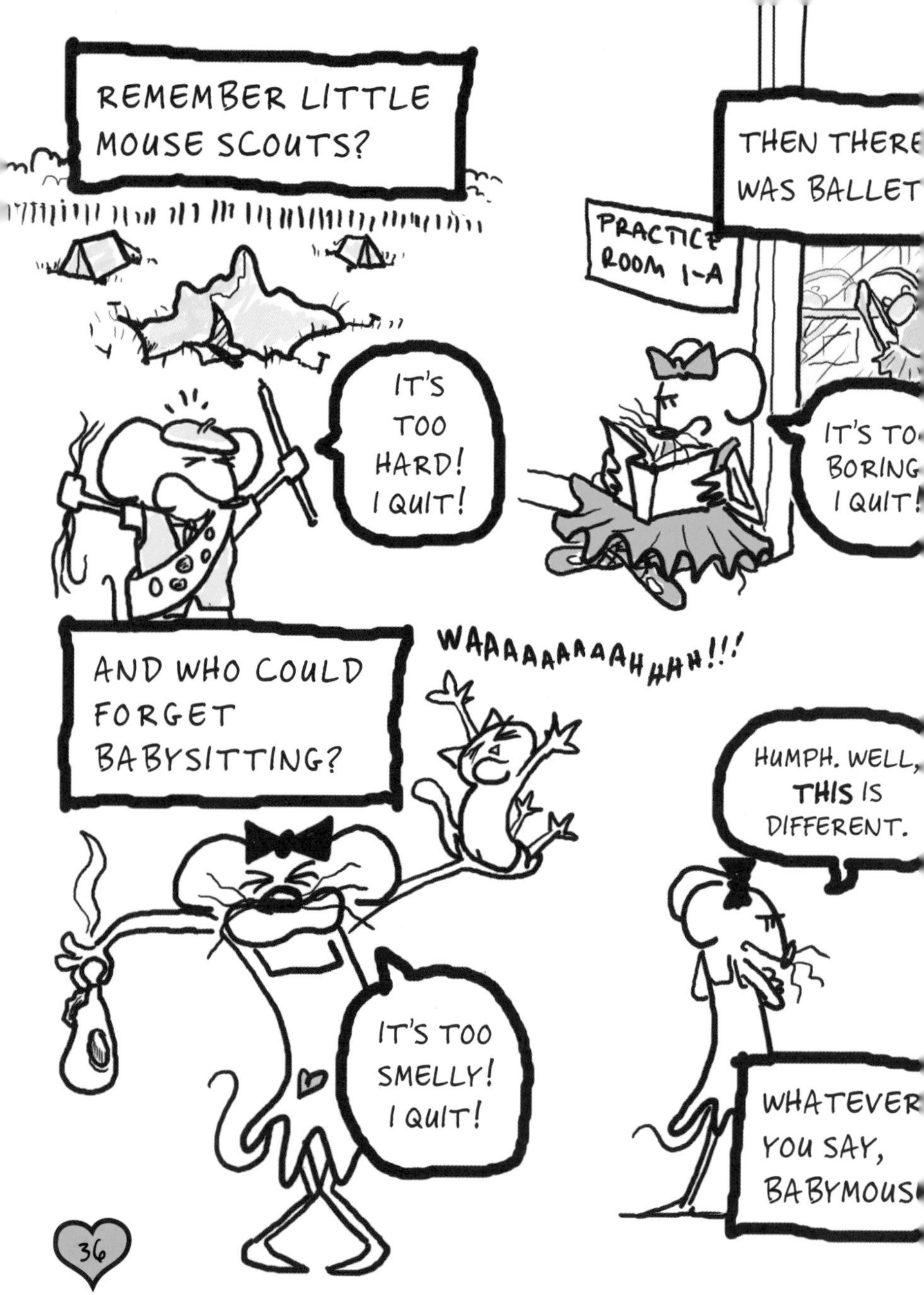
REMEMBER LITTLE MOUSE SCOUTS?
IT'S TOO HARD! I QUIT!
THEN THERE WAS BALLET
PRACTICE ROOM 1-A
IT'S TOO BORING I QUIT!
AND WHO COULD FORGET BABYSITTING?
WAAAAAAAAAHHHH!!!
IT'S TOO SMELLY! I QUIT!
HUMPH. WELL, **THIS** IS DIFFERENT.
WHATEVER YOU SAY, BABYMOUSE

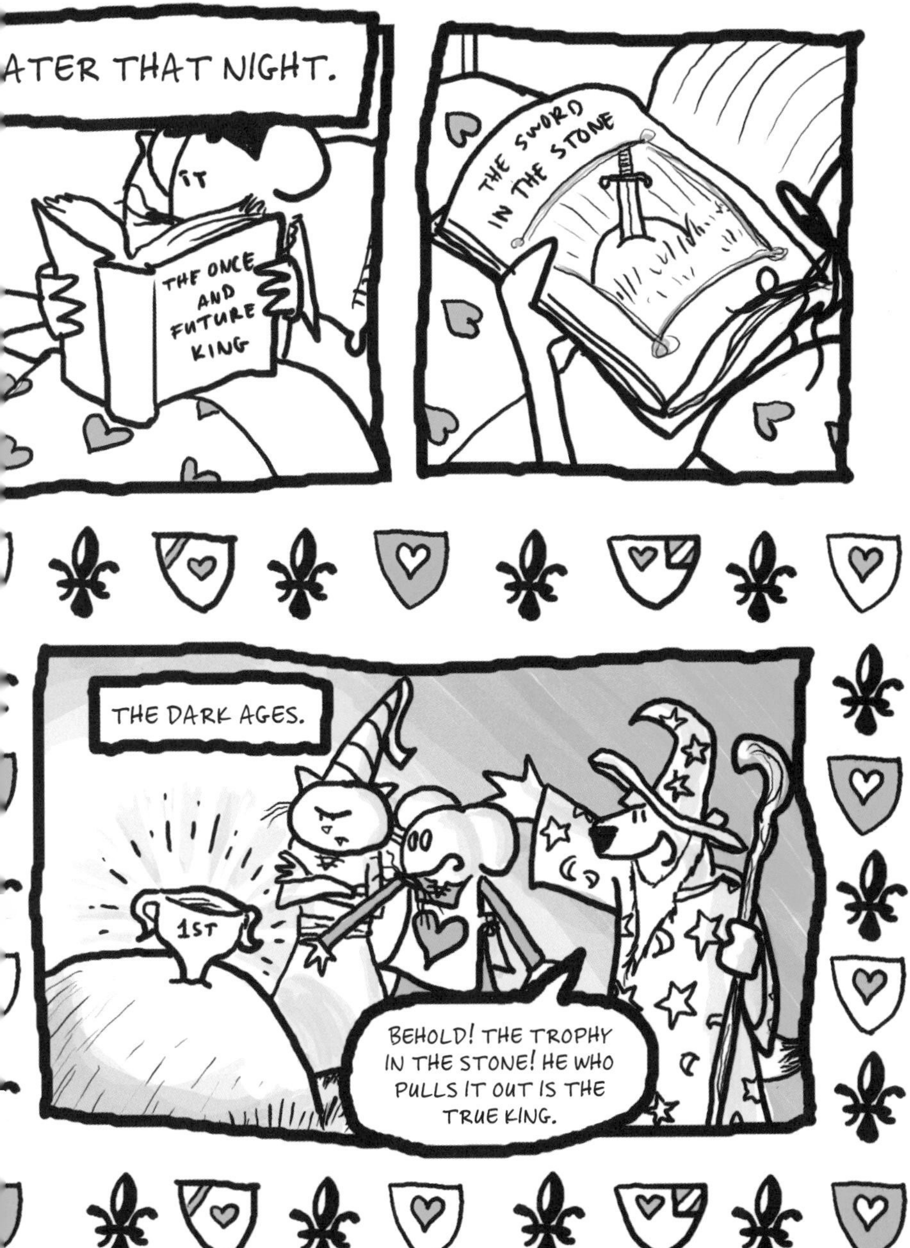
ATER THAT NIGHT.
THE ONCE AND FUTURE KING
THE SWORD IN THE STONE
THE DARK AGES.
1ST
BEHOLD! THE TROPHY IN THE STONE! HE WHO PULLS IT OUT IS THE TRUE KING.

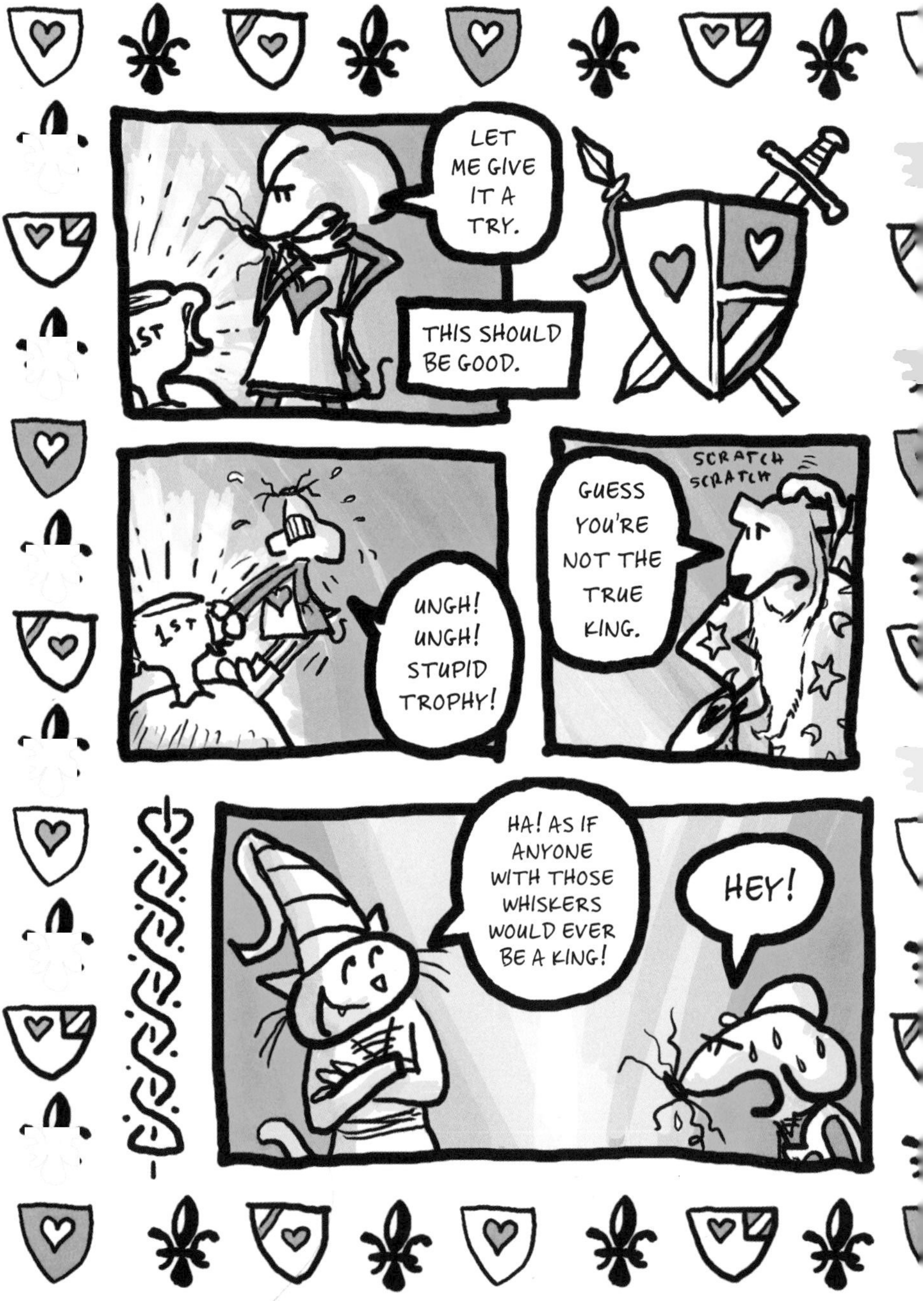
LET ME GIVE IT A TRY.
THIS SHOULD BE GOOD.
1ST
UNGH! UNGH! STUPID TROPHY!
1ST
SCRATCH SCRATCH
GUESS YOU'RE NOT THE TRUE KING.
HA! AS IF ANYONE WITH THOSE WHISKERS WOULD EVER BE A KING!
HEY!

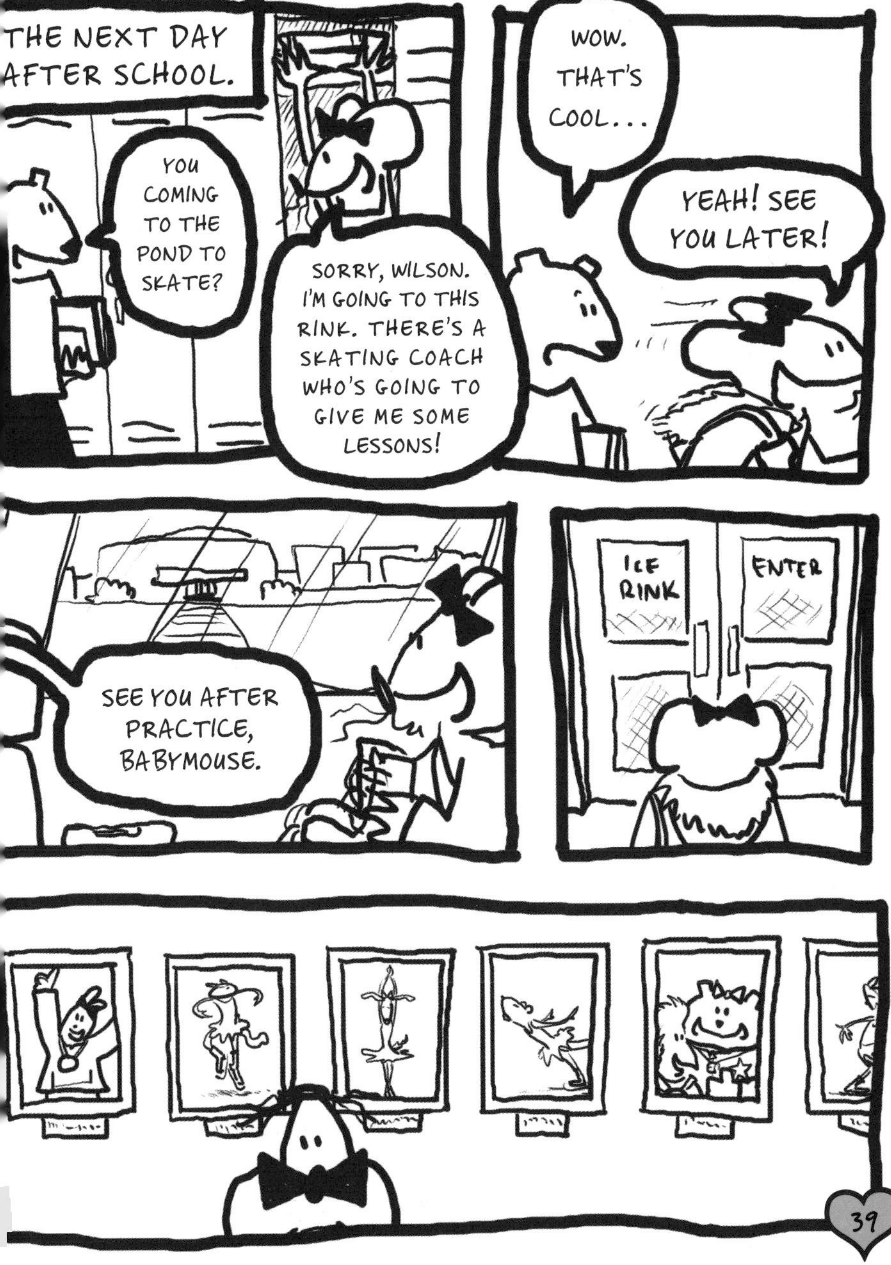
THE NEXT DAY AFTER SCHOOL.
YOU COMING TO THE POND TO SKATE?
SORRY, WILSON. I'M GOING TO THIS RINK. THERE'S A SKATING COACH WHO'S GOING TO GIVE ME SOME LESSONS!
WOW. THAT'S COOL...
YEAH! SEE YOU LATER!
SEE YOU AFTER PRACTICE, BABYMOUSE.
ICE RINK
ENTER

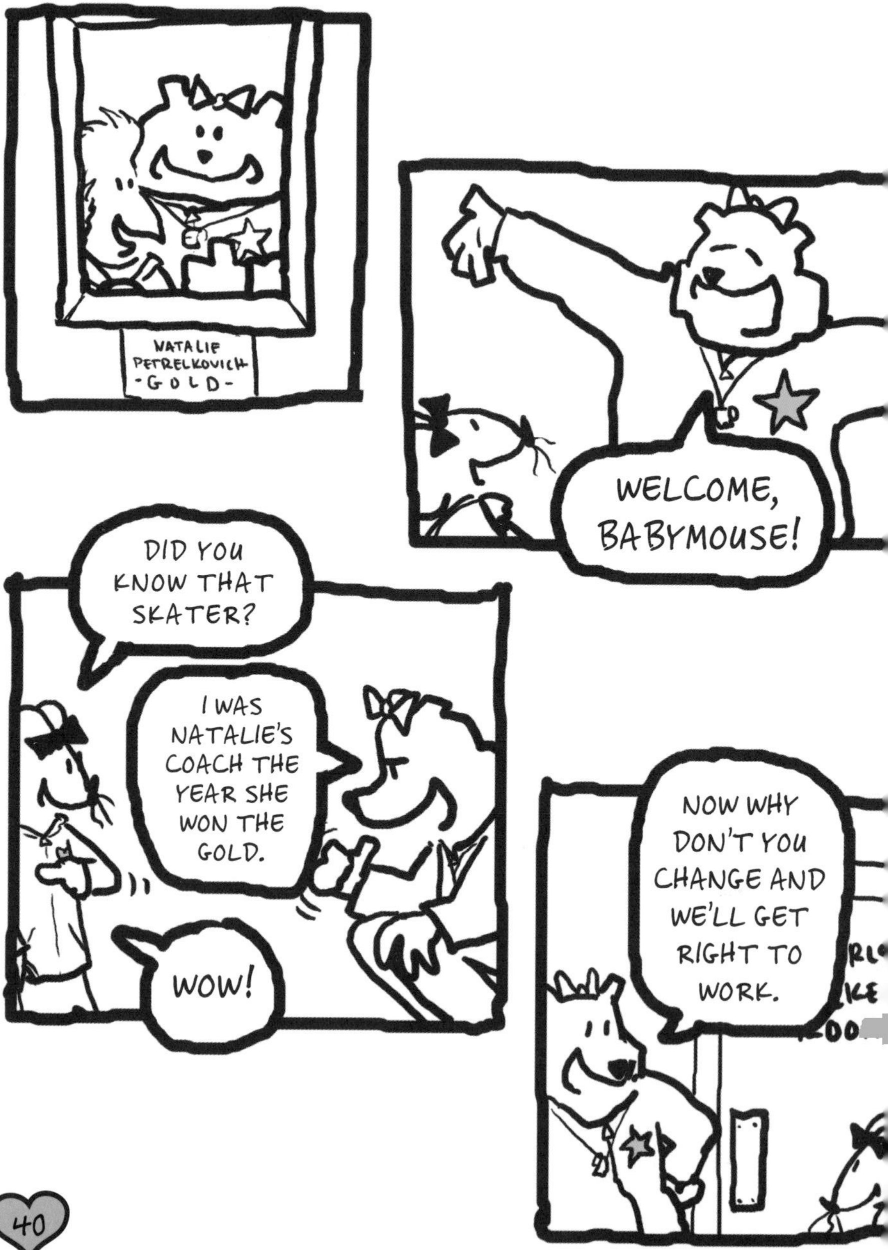
NATALIE PETRELKOVICH -GOLD-
WELCOME, BABYMOUSE!
DID YOU KNOW THAT SKATER?
I WAS NATALIE'S COACH THE YEAR SHE WON THE GOLD.
WOW!
NOW WHY DON'T YOU CHANGE AND WE'LL GET RIGHT TO WORK.

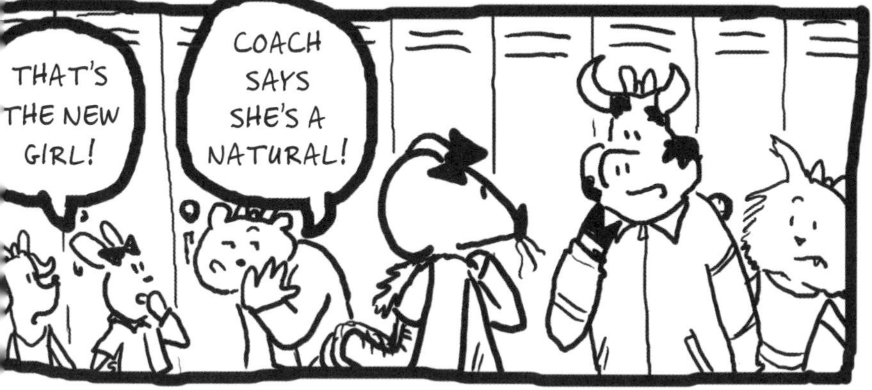
THAT'S THE NEW GIRL!
COACH SAYS SHE'S A NATURAL!

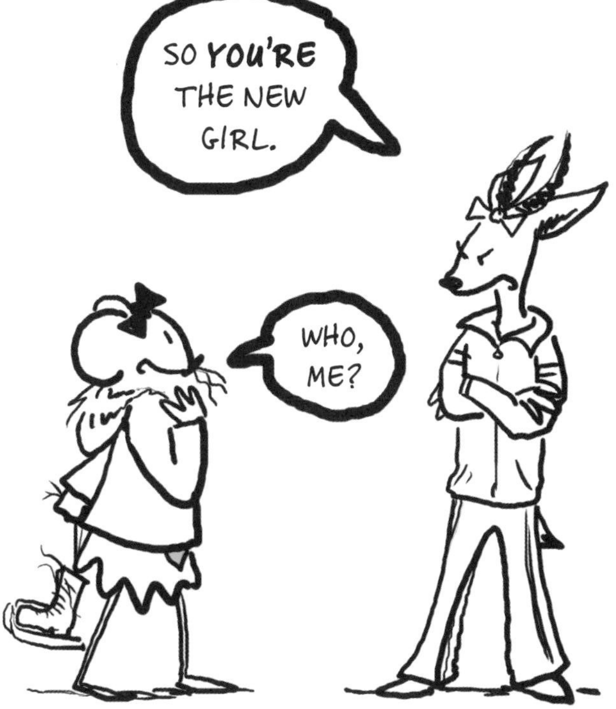
SO **YOU'RE** THE NEW GIRL.
WHO, ME?

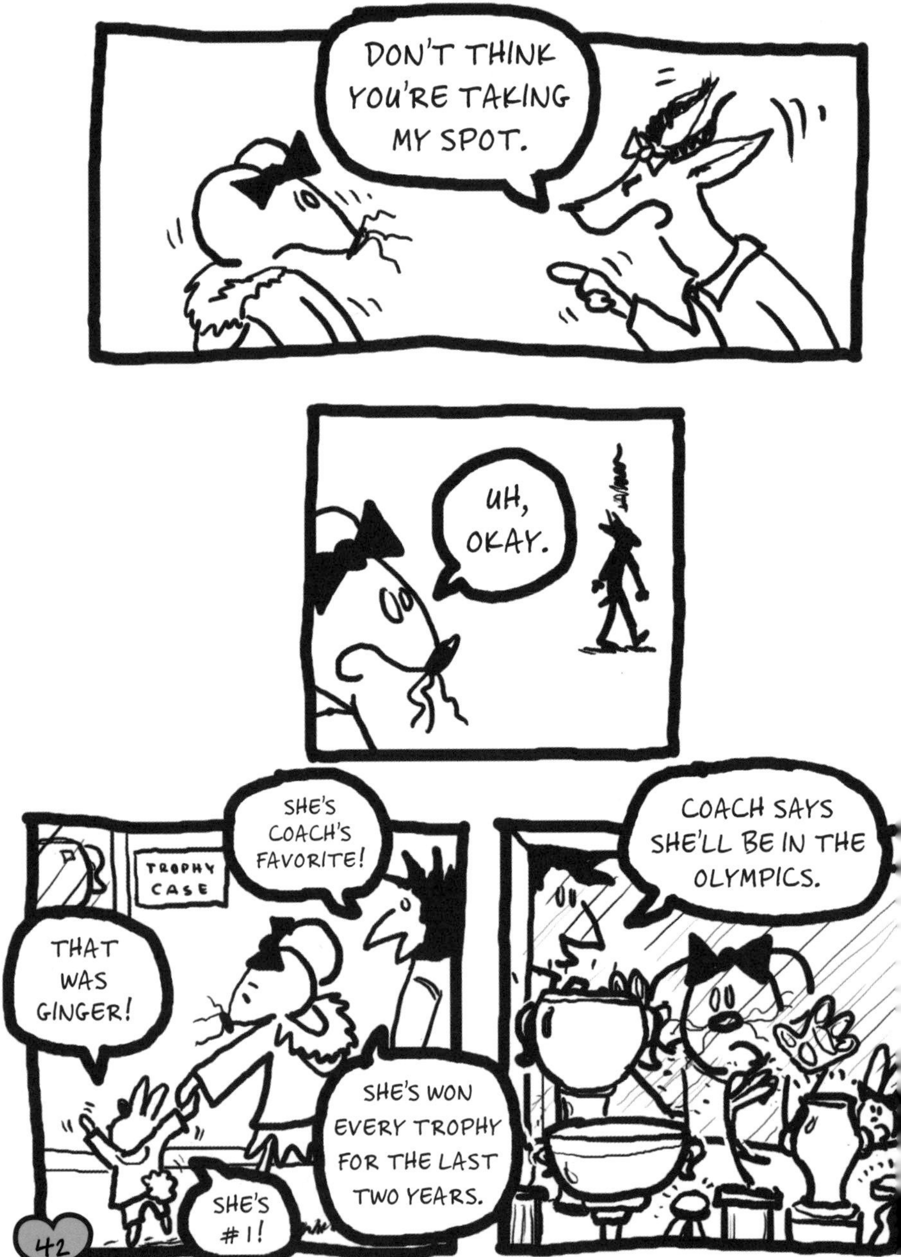

DON'T THINK YOU'RE TAKING MY SPOT.
UH, OKAY.
SHE'S COACH'S FAVORITE!
TROPHY CASE
THAT WAS GINGER!
SHE'S WON EVERY TROPHY FOR THE LAST TWO YEARS.
SHE'S #1!
COACH SAYS SHE'LL BE IN THE OLYMPICS.

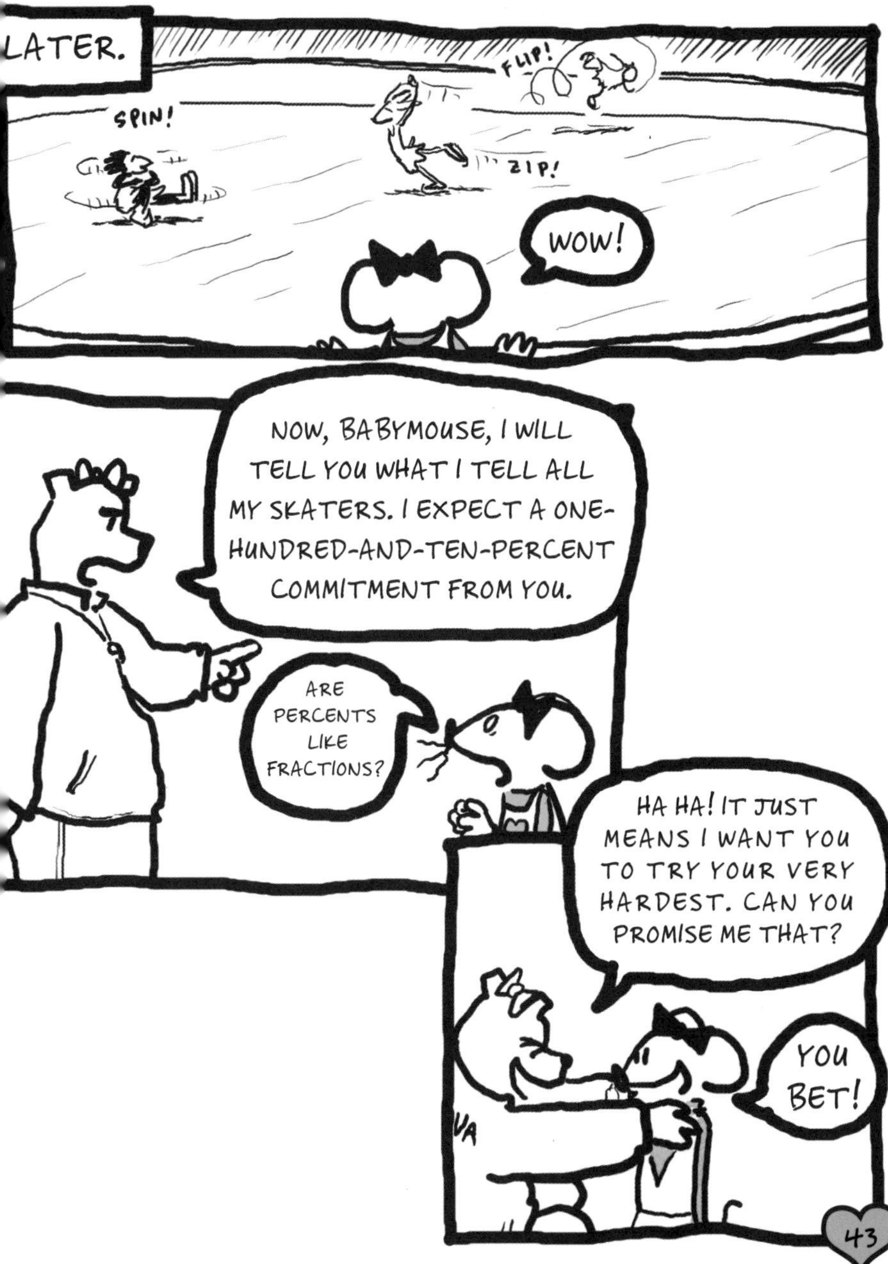
LATER.
SPIN!
FLIP!
ZIP!
WOW!
NOW, BABYMOUSE, I WILL TELL YOU WHAT I TELL ALL MY SKATERS. I EXPECT A ONE-HUNDRED-AND-TEN-PERCENT COMMITMENT FROM YOU.
ARE PERCENTS LIKE FRACTIONS?
HA HA! IT JUST MEANS I WANT YOU TO TRY YOUR VERY HARDEST. CAN YOU PROMISE ME THAT?
YOU BET!

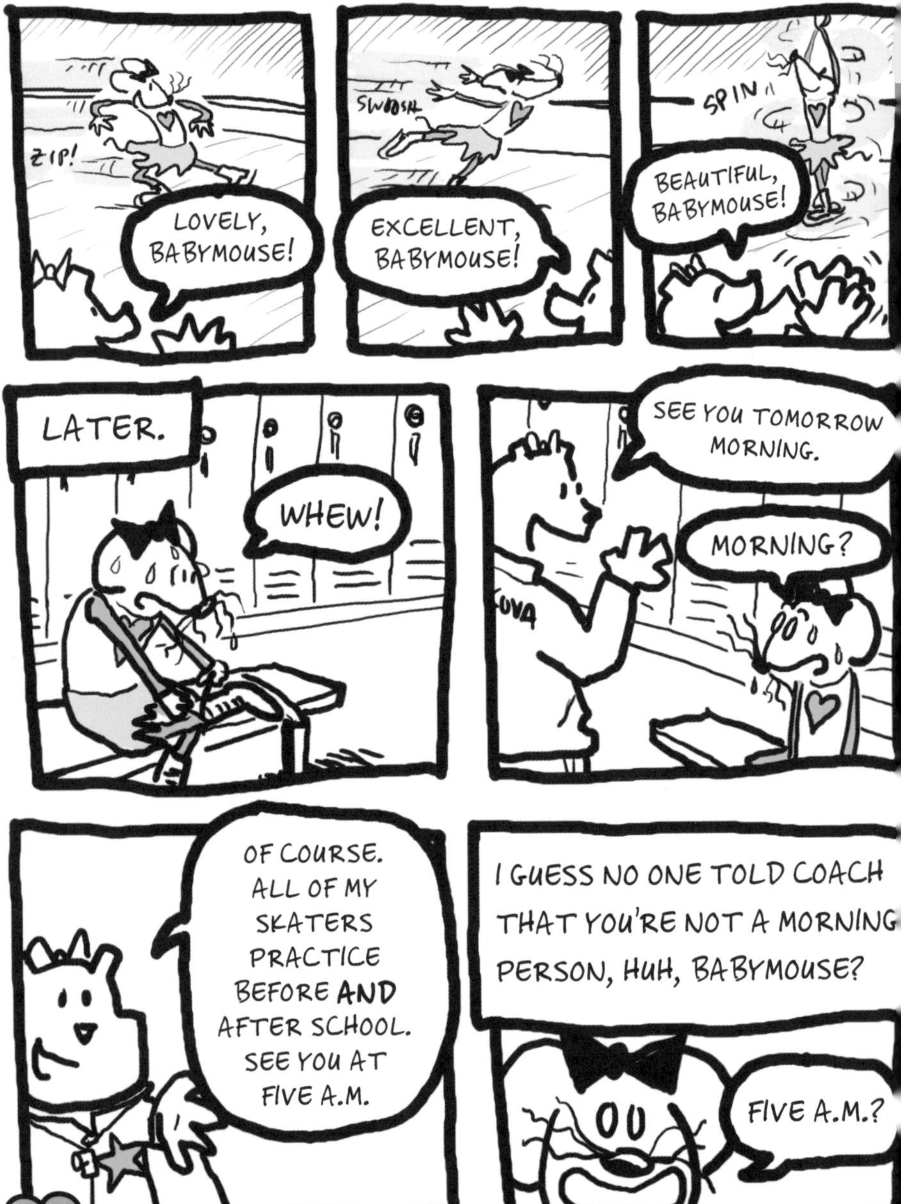
ZIP!
LOVELY, BABYMOUSE!
SWOOSH
EXCELLENT, BABYMOUSE!
SPIN
BEAUTIFUL, BABYMOUSE!
LATER.
WHEW!
SEE YOU TOMORROW MORNING.
MORNING?
OF COURSE. ALL OF MY SKATERS PRACTICE BEFORE **AND** AFTER SCHOOL. SEE YOU AT FIVE A.M.
I GUESS NO ONE TOLD COACH THAT YOU'RE NOT A MORNING PERSON, HUH, BABYMOUSE?
FIVE A.M.?

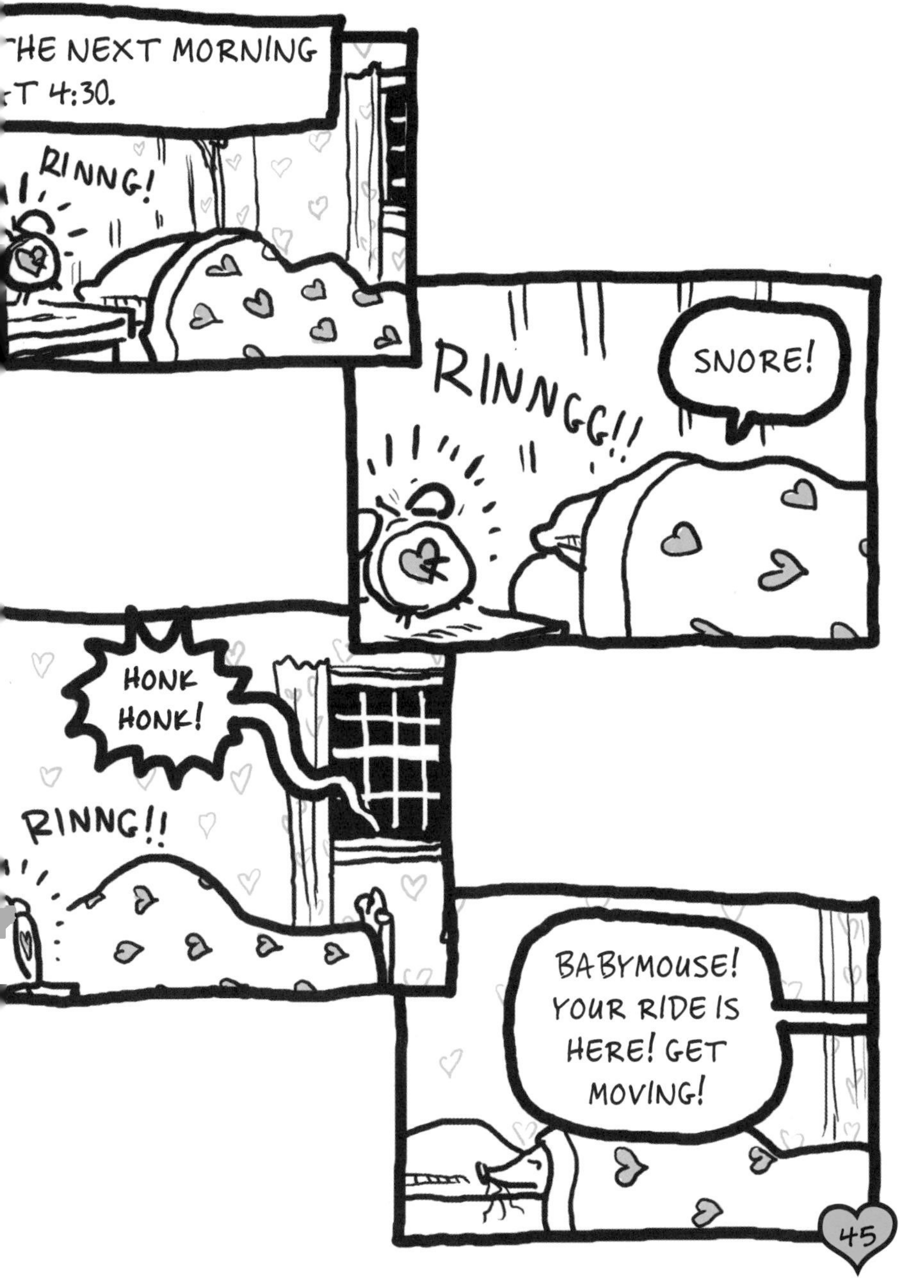

HE NEXT MORNING
T 4:30.
RINNG!
RINNGG!!
SNORE!
HONK
HONK!
RINNG!!
BABYMOUSE! YOUR RIDE IS HERE! GET MOVING!

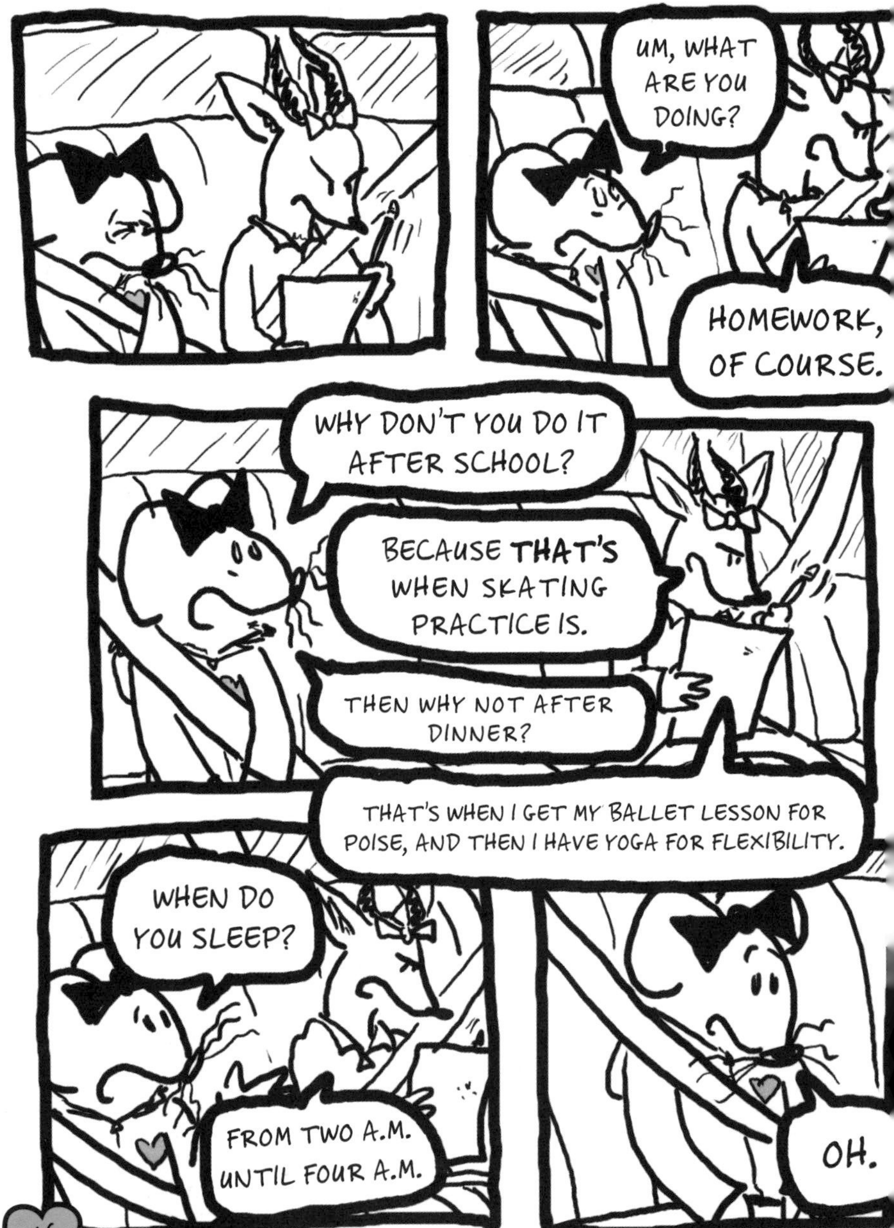
UM, WHAT ARE YOU DOING?
HOMEWORK, OF COURSE.
WHY DON'T YOU DO IT AFTER SCHOOL?
BECAUSE **THAT'S** WHEN SKATING PRACTICE IS.
THEN WHY NOT AFTER DINNER?
THAT'S WHEN I GET MY BALLET LESSON FOR POISE, AND THEN I HAVE YOGA FOR FLEXIBILITY.
WHEN DO YOU SLEEP?
FROM TWO A.M. UNTIL FOUR A.M.
OH.

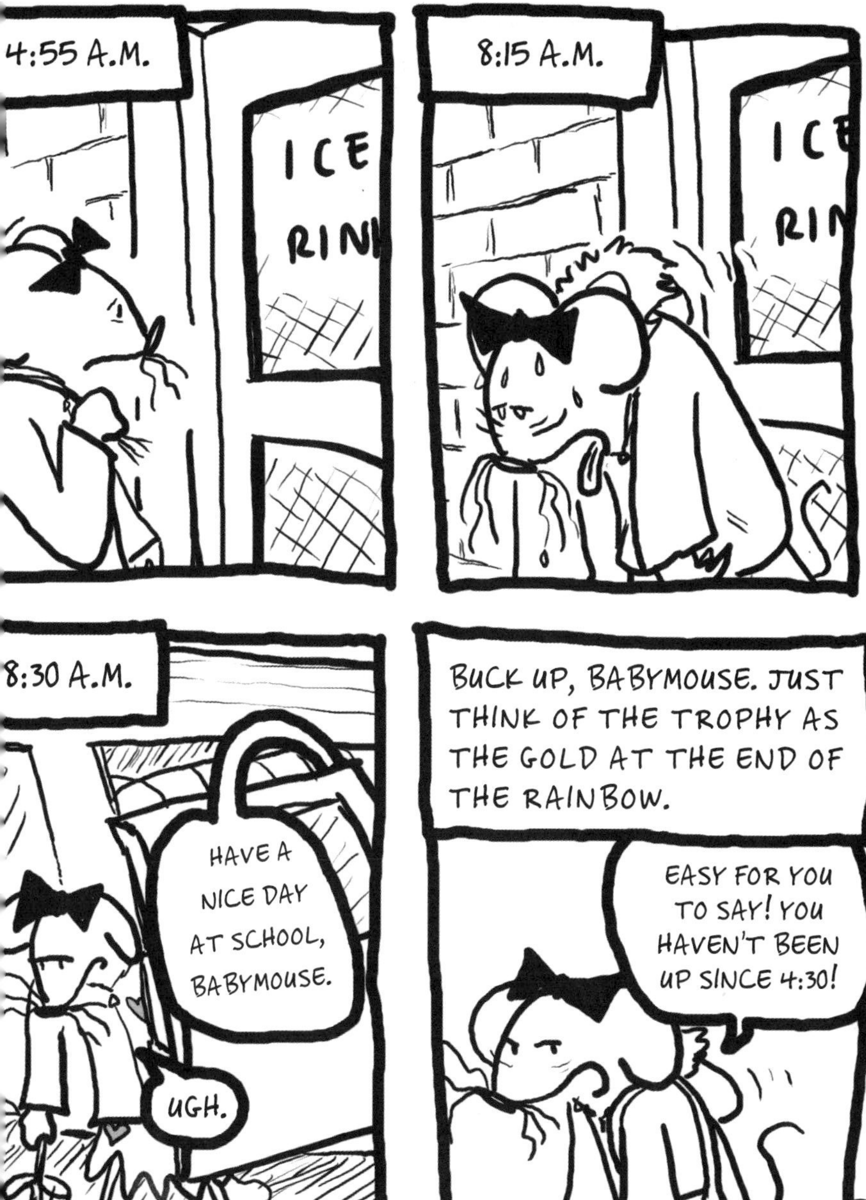
4:55 A.M.
ICE RINK
8:15 A.M.
ICE RIN
8:30 A.M.
HAVE A NICE DAY AT SCHOOL, BABYMOUSE.
UGH.
BUCK UP, BABYMOUSE. JUST THINK OF THE TROPHY AS THE GOLD AT THE END OF THE RAINBOW.
EASY FOR YOU TO SAY! YOU HAVEN'T BEEN UP SINCE 4:30!

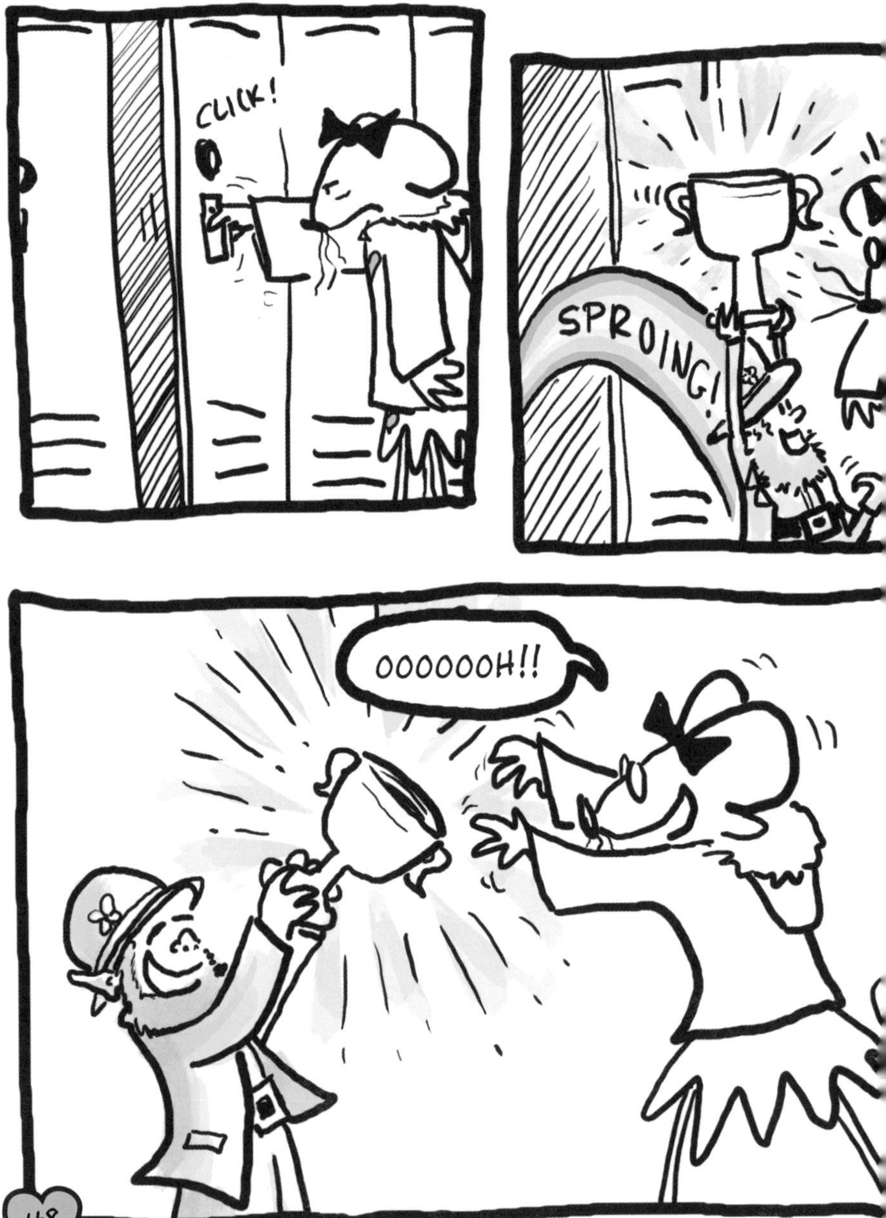
CLICK!
SPROING!
OOOOOOH!!

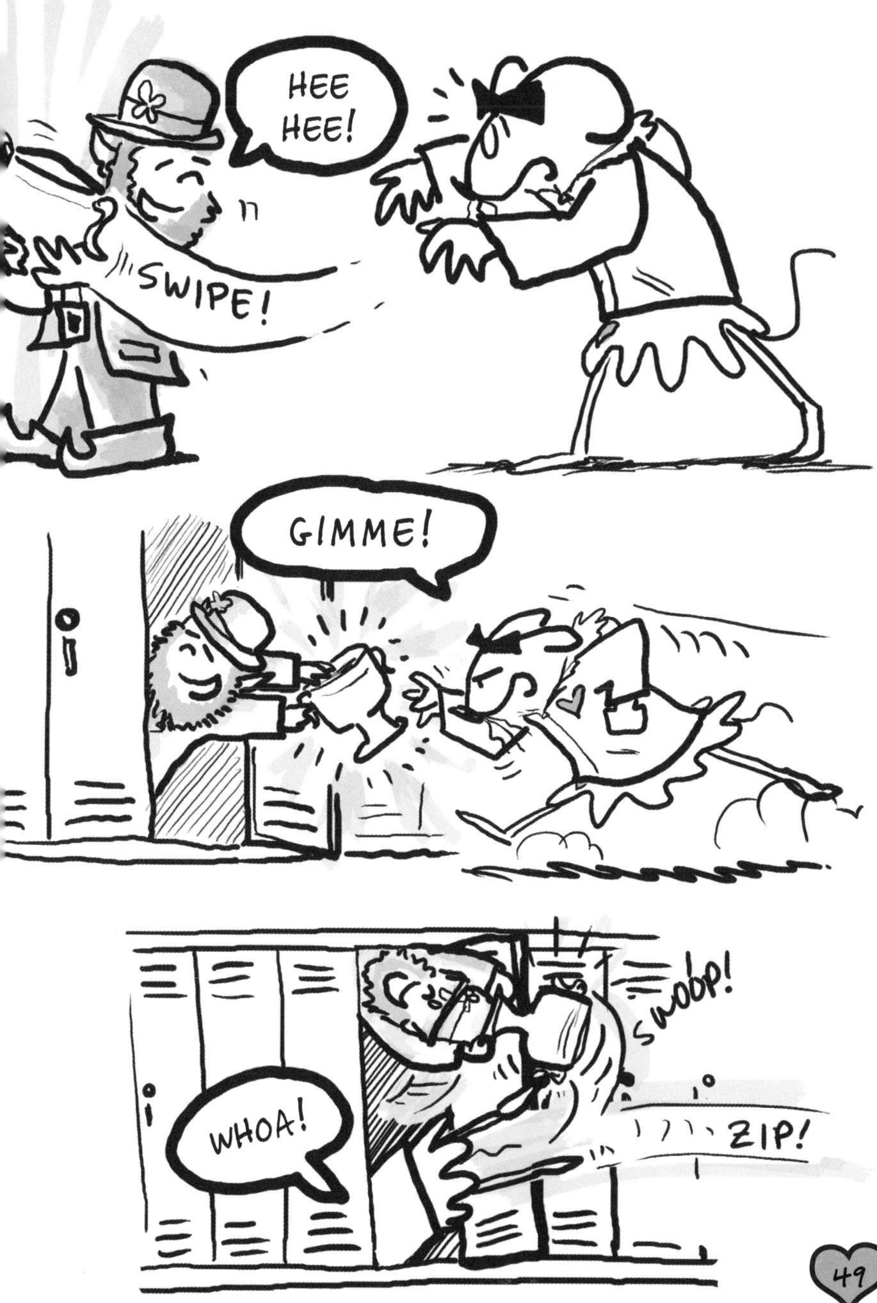
HEE HEE!
SWIPE!
GIMME!
SWOOP!
WHOA!
ZIP!

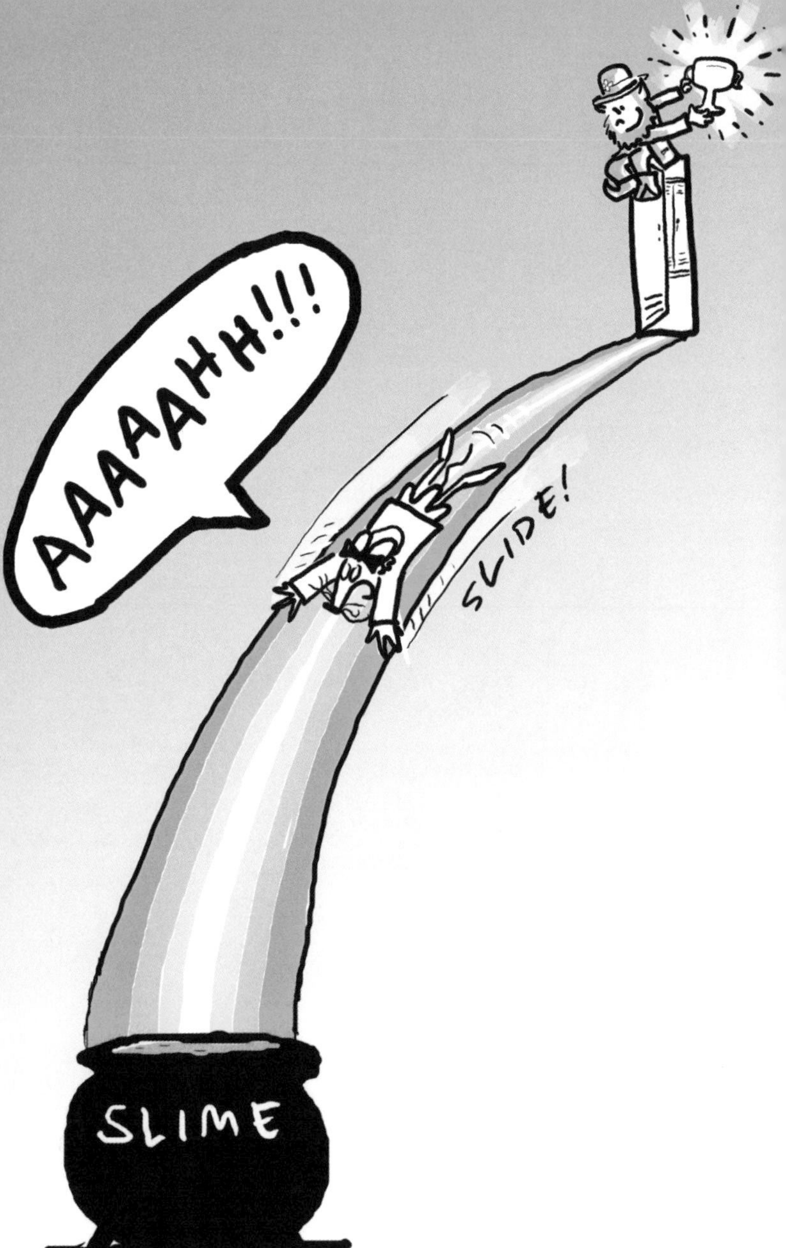
AAAAAHH!!!
SLIDE!
SLIME

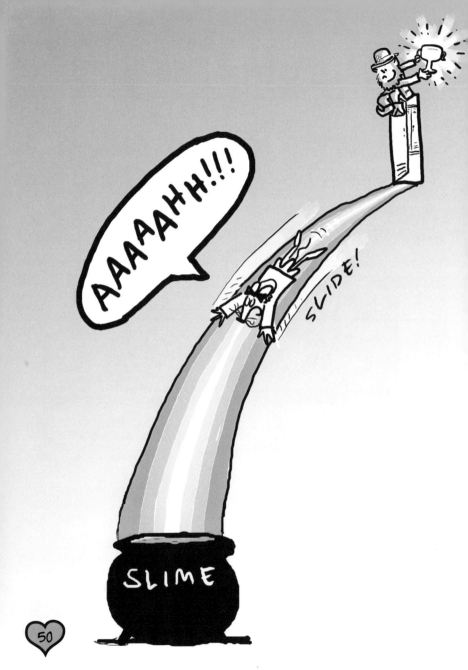

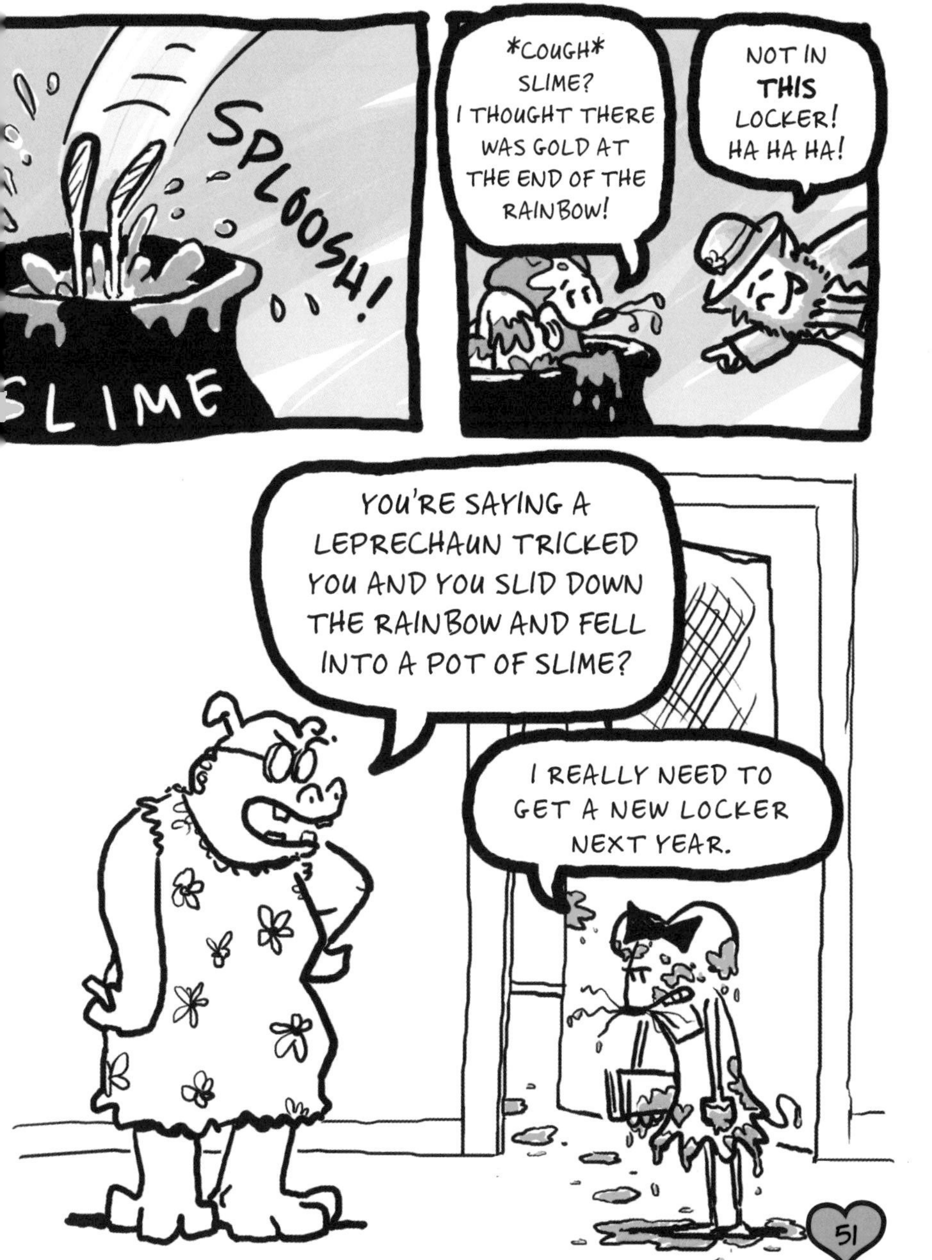
SPLOOSH!
SLIME
COUGH SLIME? I THOUGHT THERE WAS GOLD AT THE END OF THE RAINBOW!
NOT IN **THIS** LOCKER! HA HA HA!
YOU'RE SAYING A LEPRECHAUN TRICKED YOU AND YOU SLID DOWN THE RAINBOW AND FELL INTO A POT OF SLIME?
I REALLY NEED TO GET A NEW LOCKER NEXT YEAR.

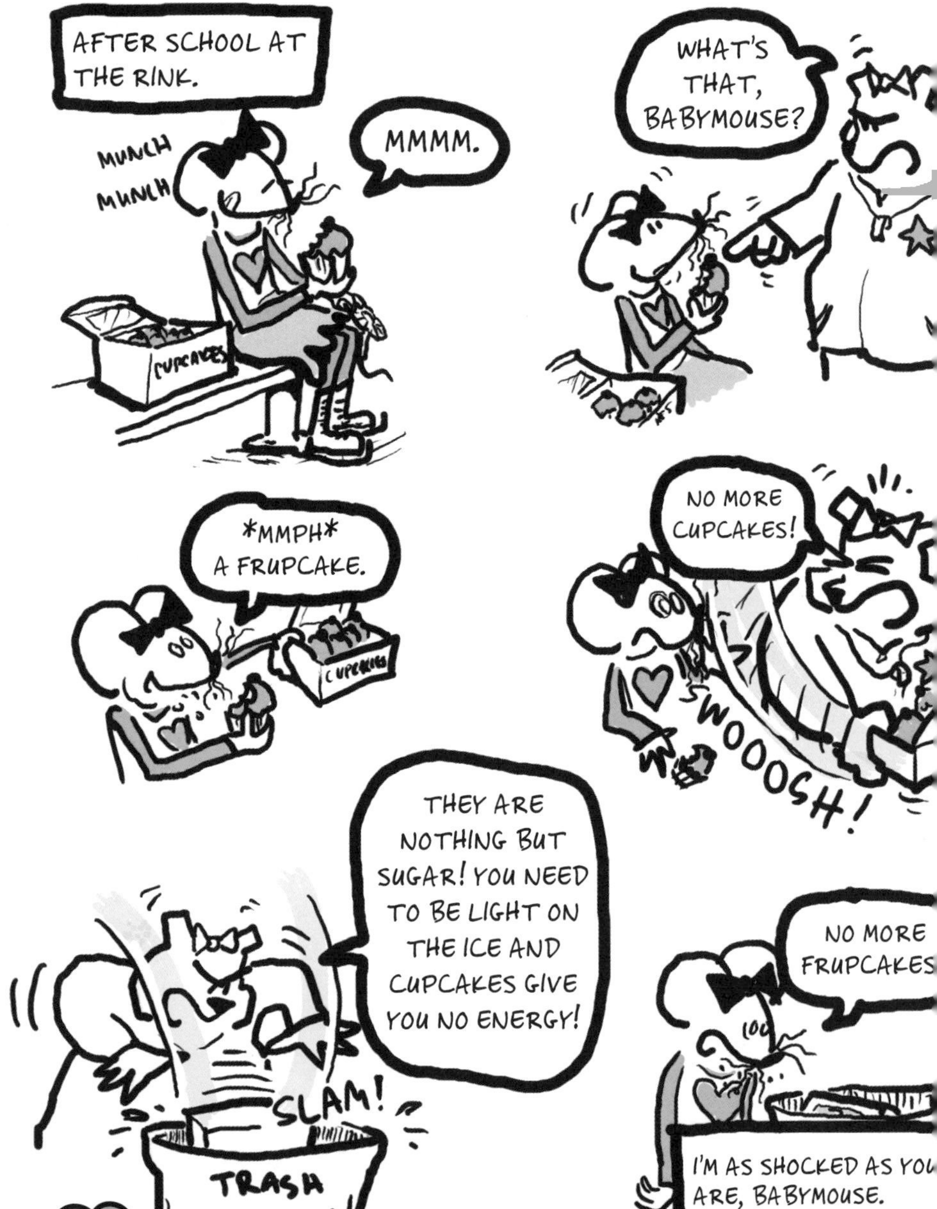
AFTER SCHOOL AT THE RINK.
MUNCH
MUNCH
MMMM.
CUPCAKES
WHAT'S THAT, BABYMOUSE?
MMPH A FRUPCAKE.
CUPCAKES
NO MORE CUPCAKES!
WOOOOSH!
THEY ARE NOTHING BUT SUGAR! YOU NEED TO BE LIGHT ON THE ICE AND CUPCAKES GIVE YOU NO ENERGY!
SLAM!
TRASH
NO MORE FRUPCAKES
I'M AS SHOCKED AS YOU ARE, BABYMOUSE.

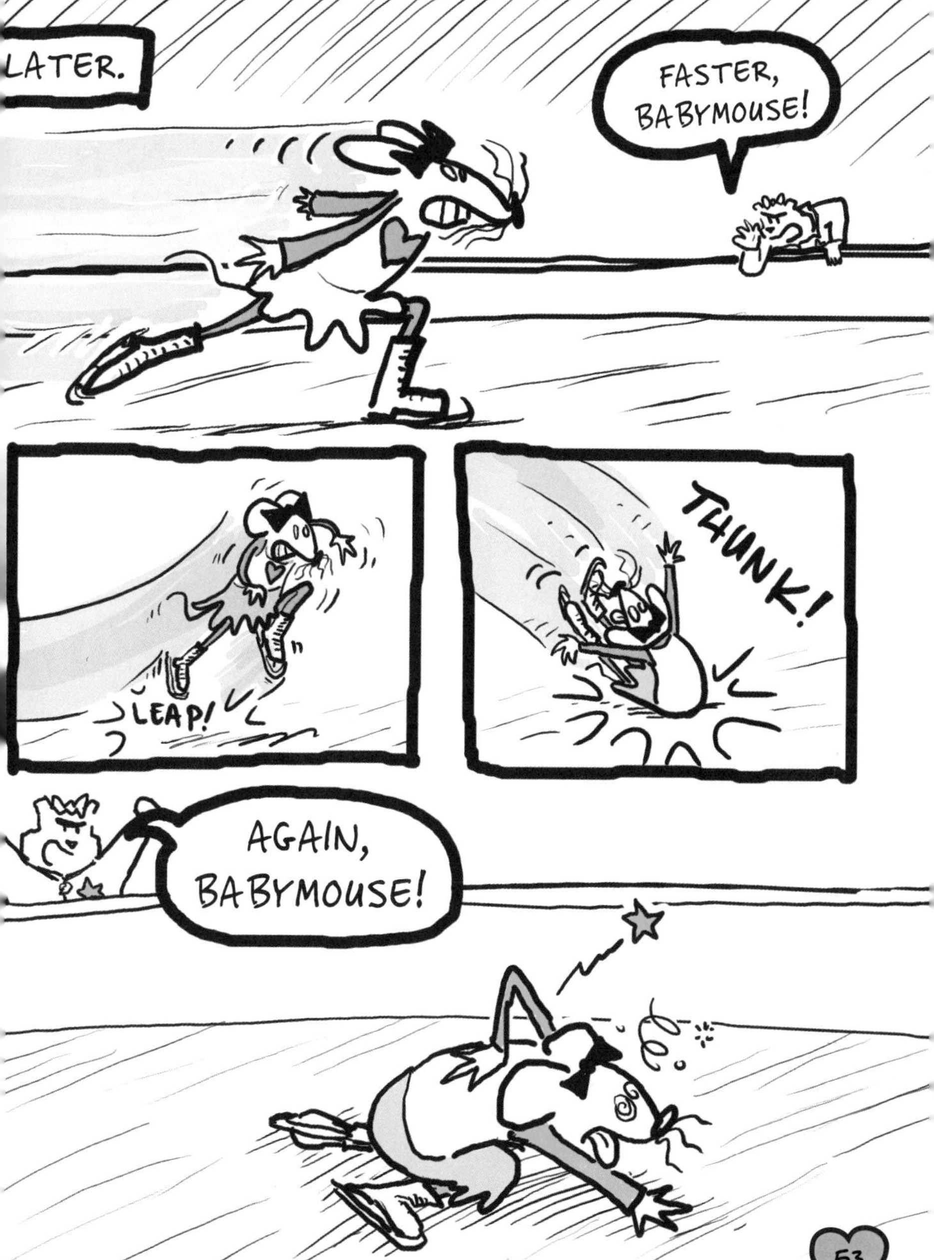
LATER.
FASTER, BABYMOUSE!
LEAP!
THUNK!
AGAIN, BABYMOUSE!

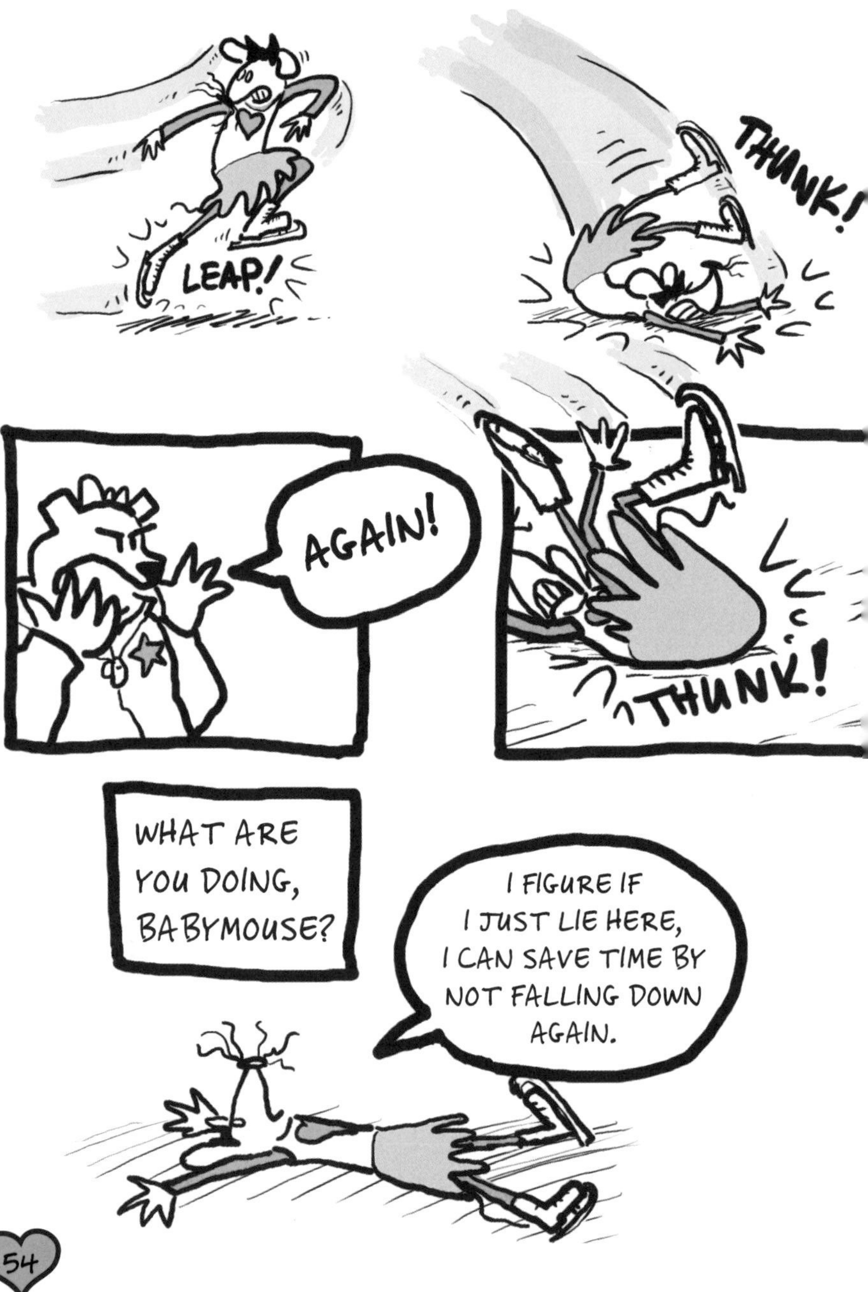
LEAP!
THUNK!
AGAIN!
THUNK!
WHAT ARE YOU DOING, BABYMOUSE?
I FIGURE IF I JUST LIE HERE, I CAN SAVE TIME BY NOT FALLING DOWN AGAIN.

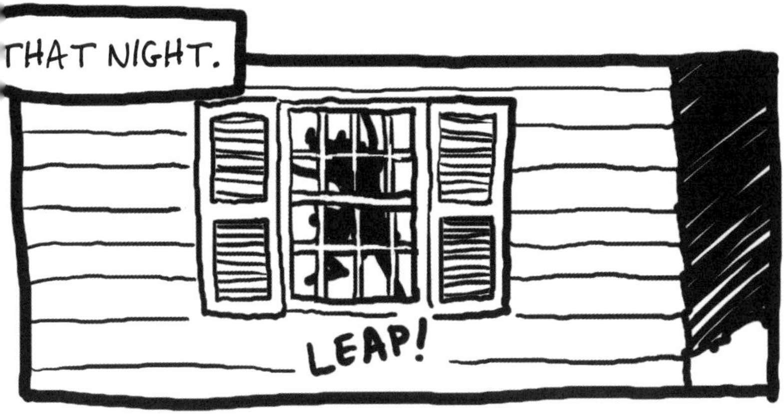
THAT NIGHT.
LEAP!

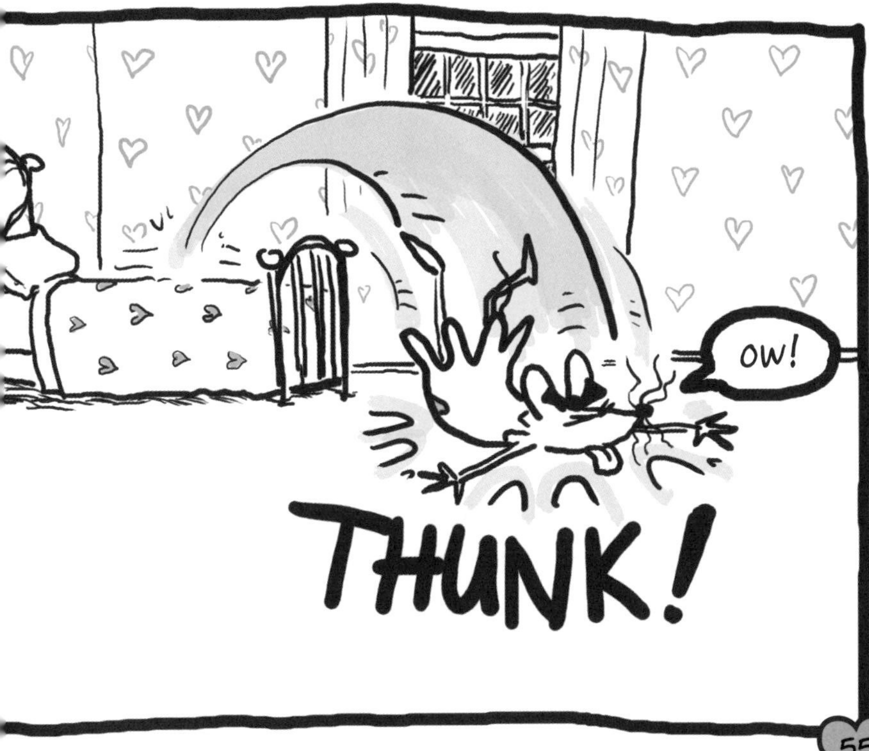
OW!
THUNK!

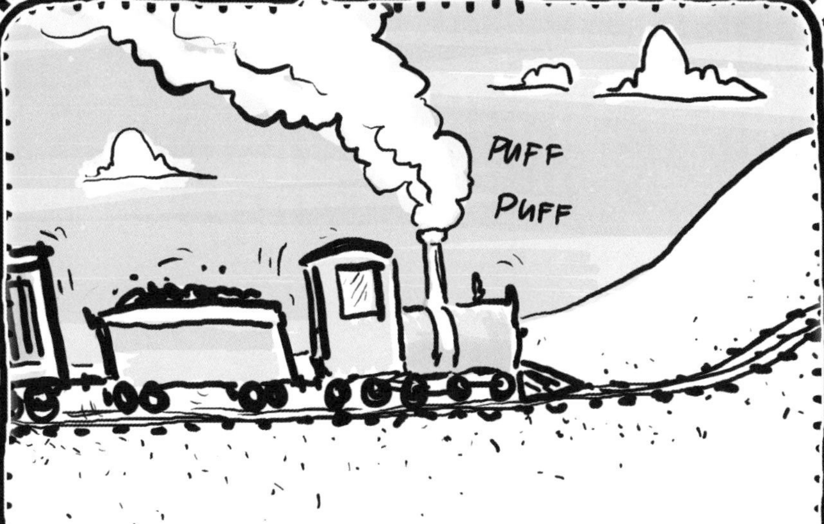
PUFF
PUFF

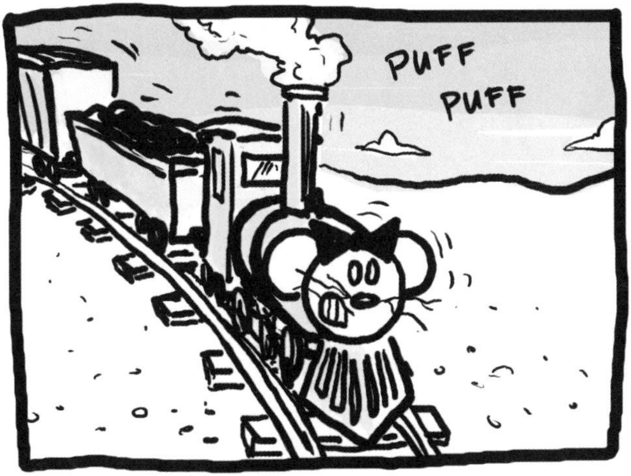
PUFF
PUFF

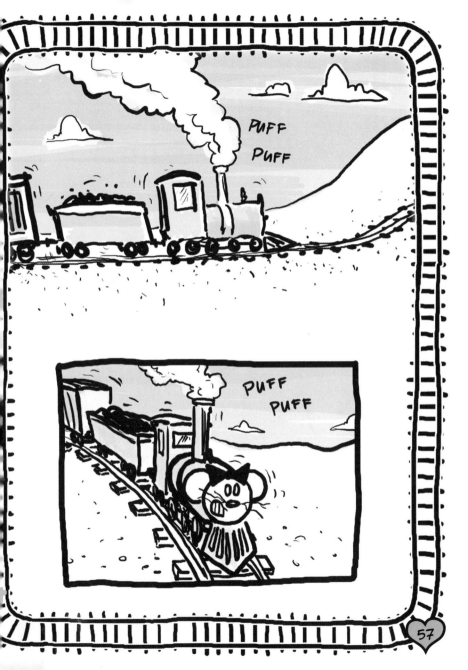

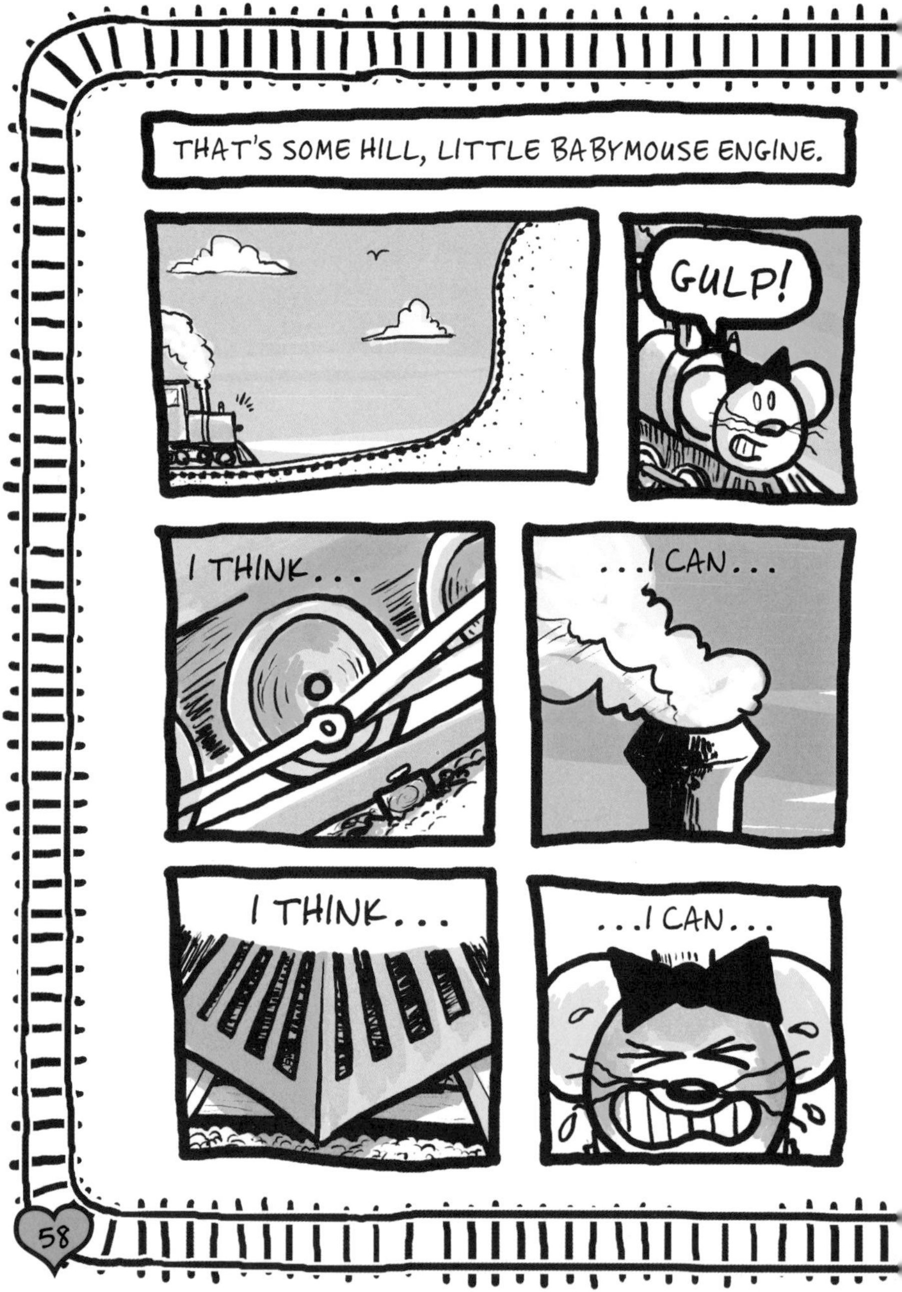
THAT'S SOME HILL, LITTLE BABYMOUSE ENGINE.
GULP!
I THINK...
...I CAN...
I THINK...
...I CAN...

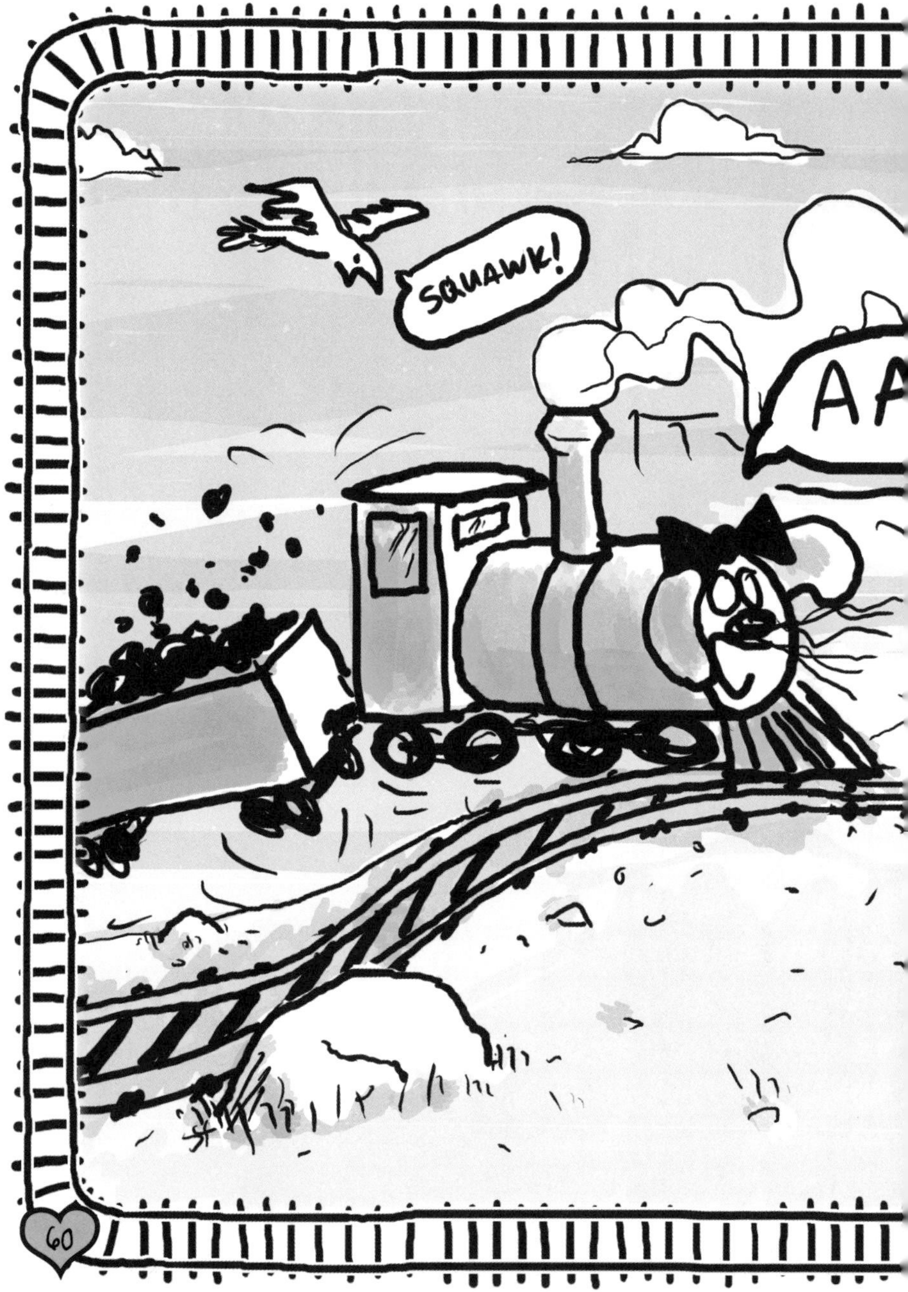
SQUAWK!
AA

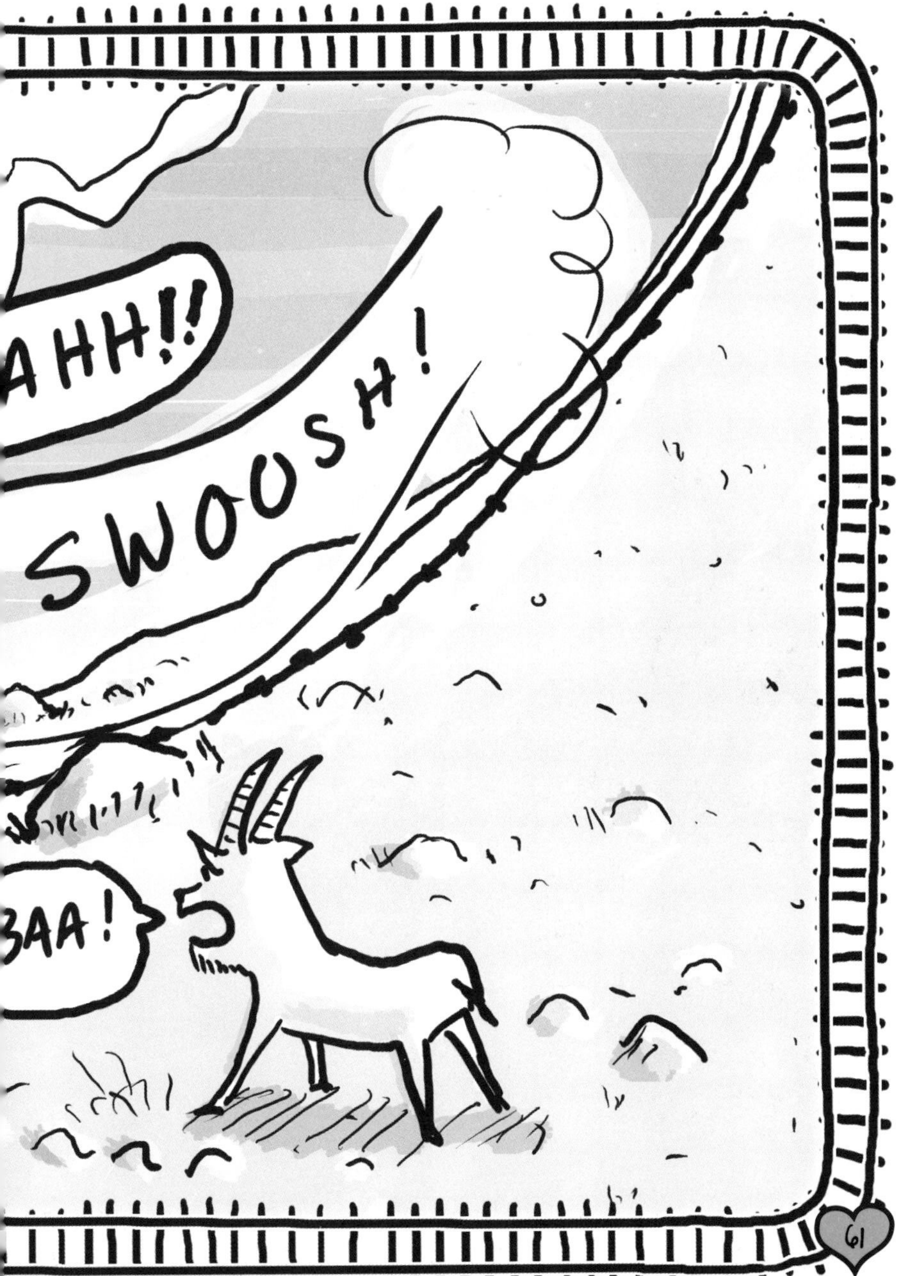
AHH!!
SWOOSH!
BAA!

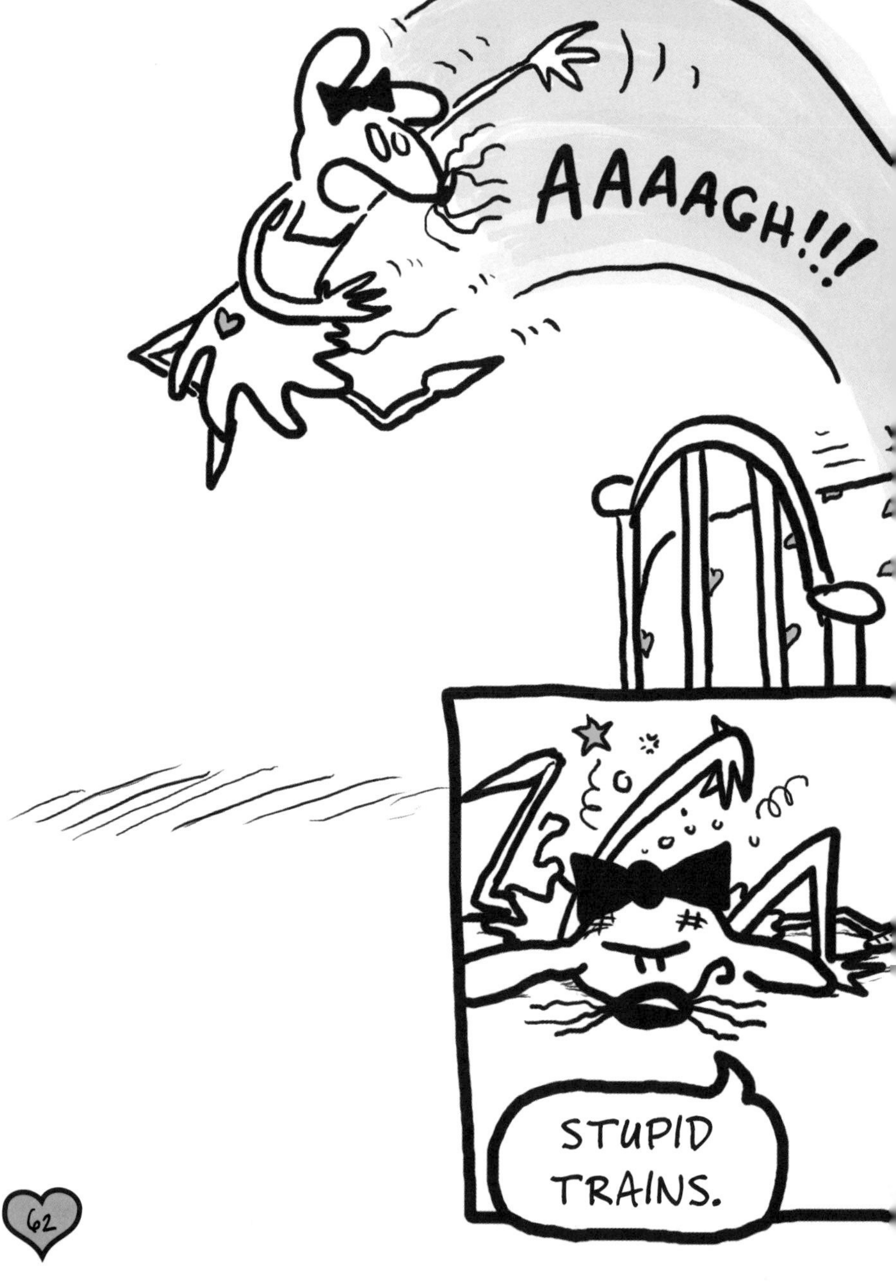
AAAAGH!!!
STUPID TRAINS.

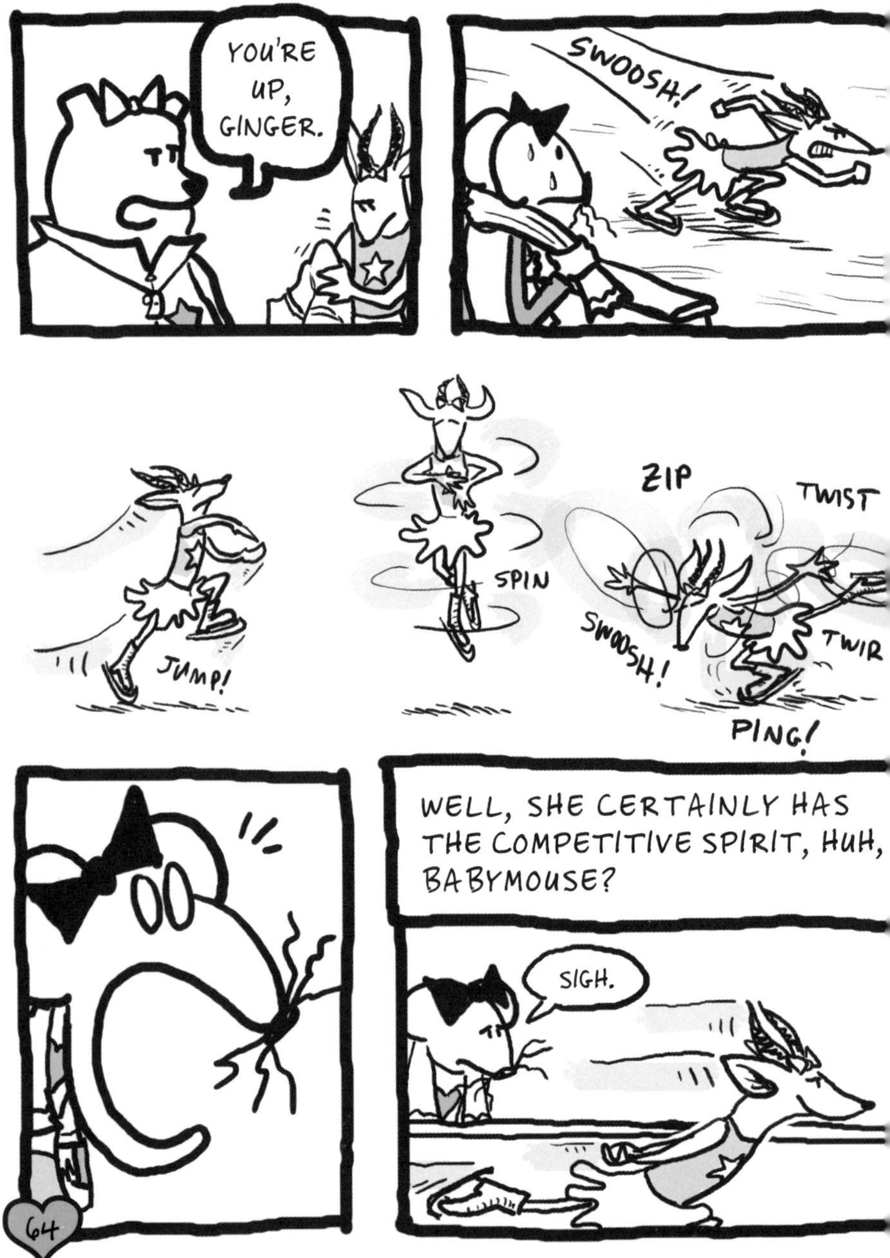

YOU'RE UP, GINGER.
SWOOSH!
ZIP
TWIST
SPIN
JUMP!
SWOOSH!
TWIR
PING!
WELL, SHE CERTAINLY HAS THE COMPETITIVE SPIRIT, HUH, BABYMOUSE?
SIGH.

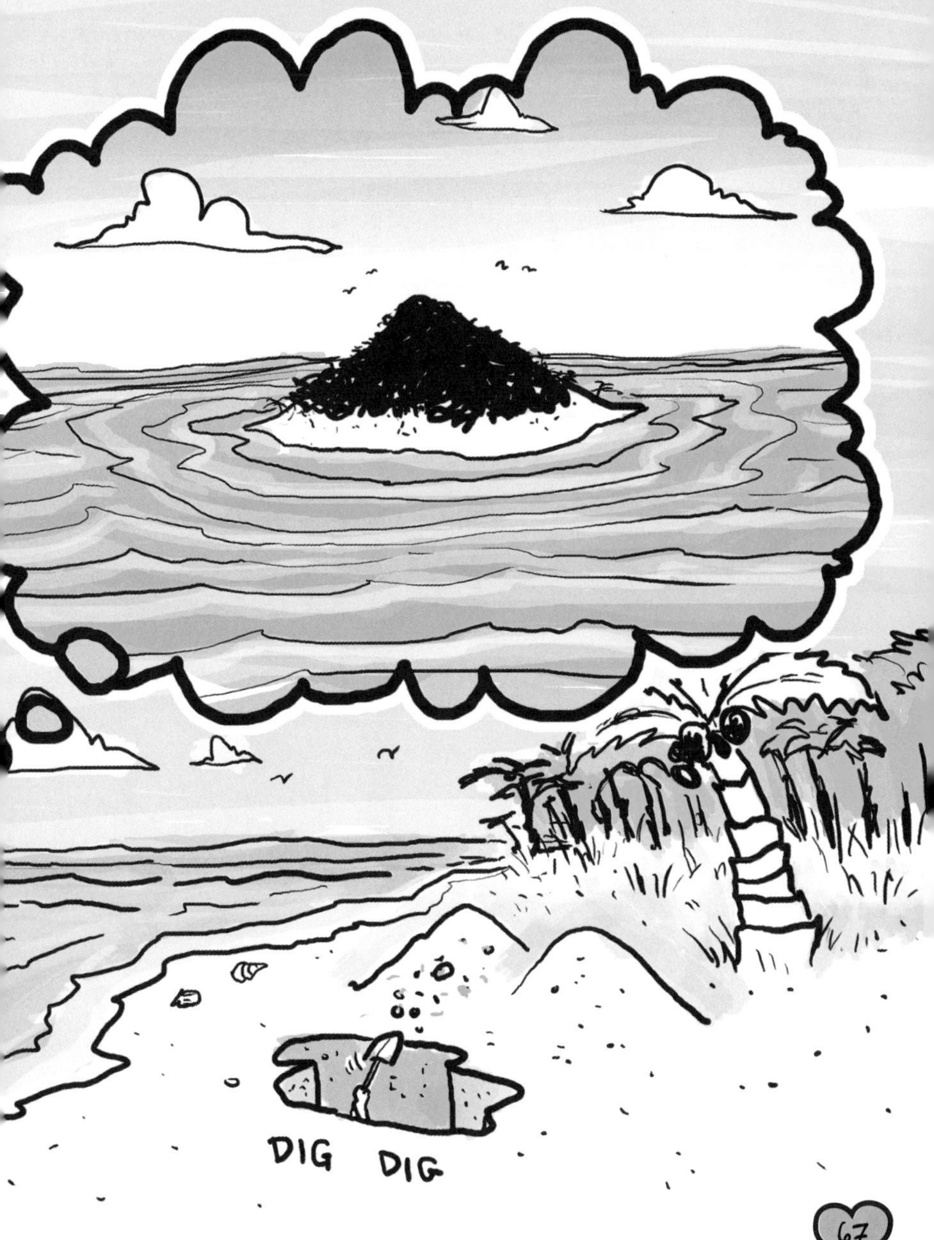
DIG DIG

73

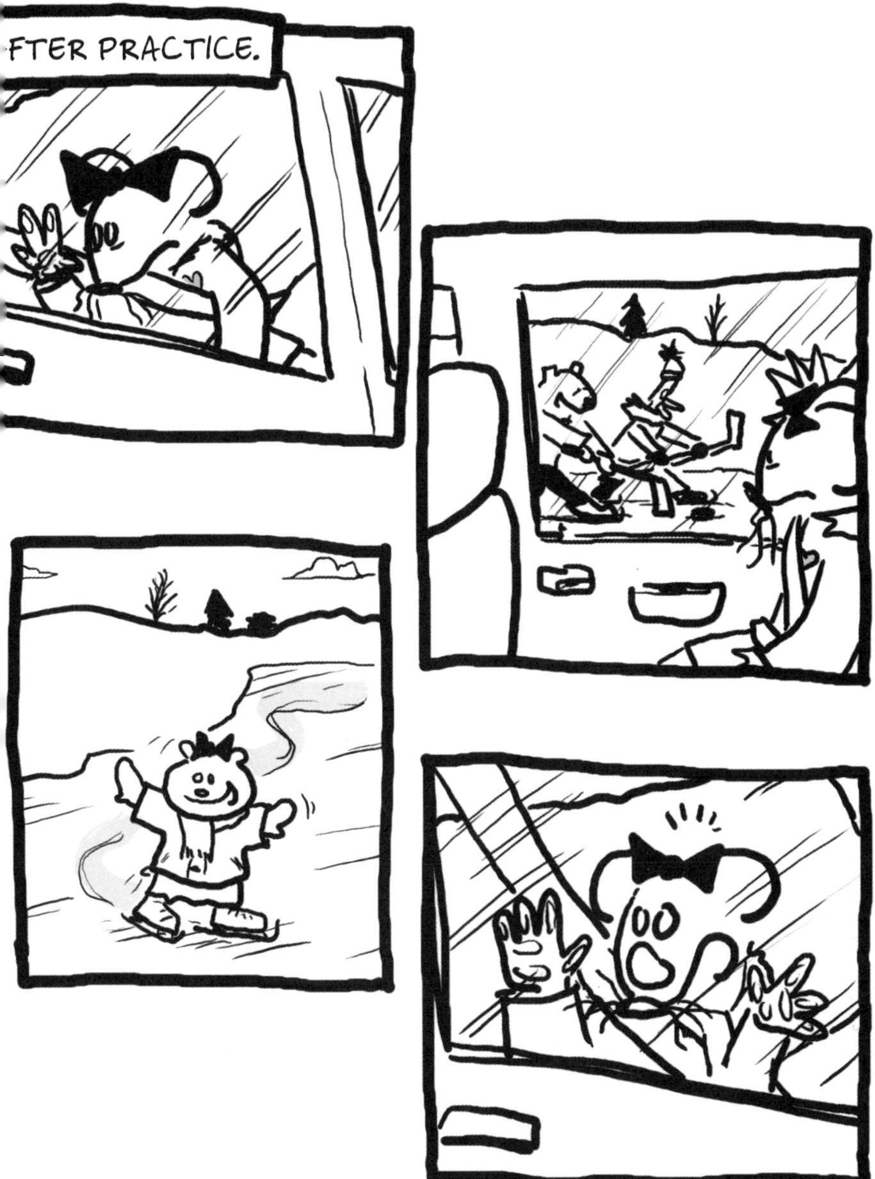
FTER PRACTICE.

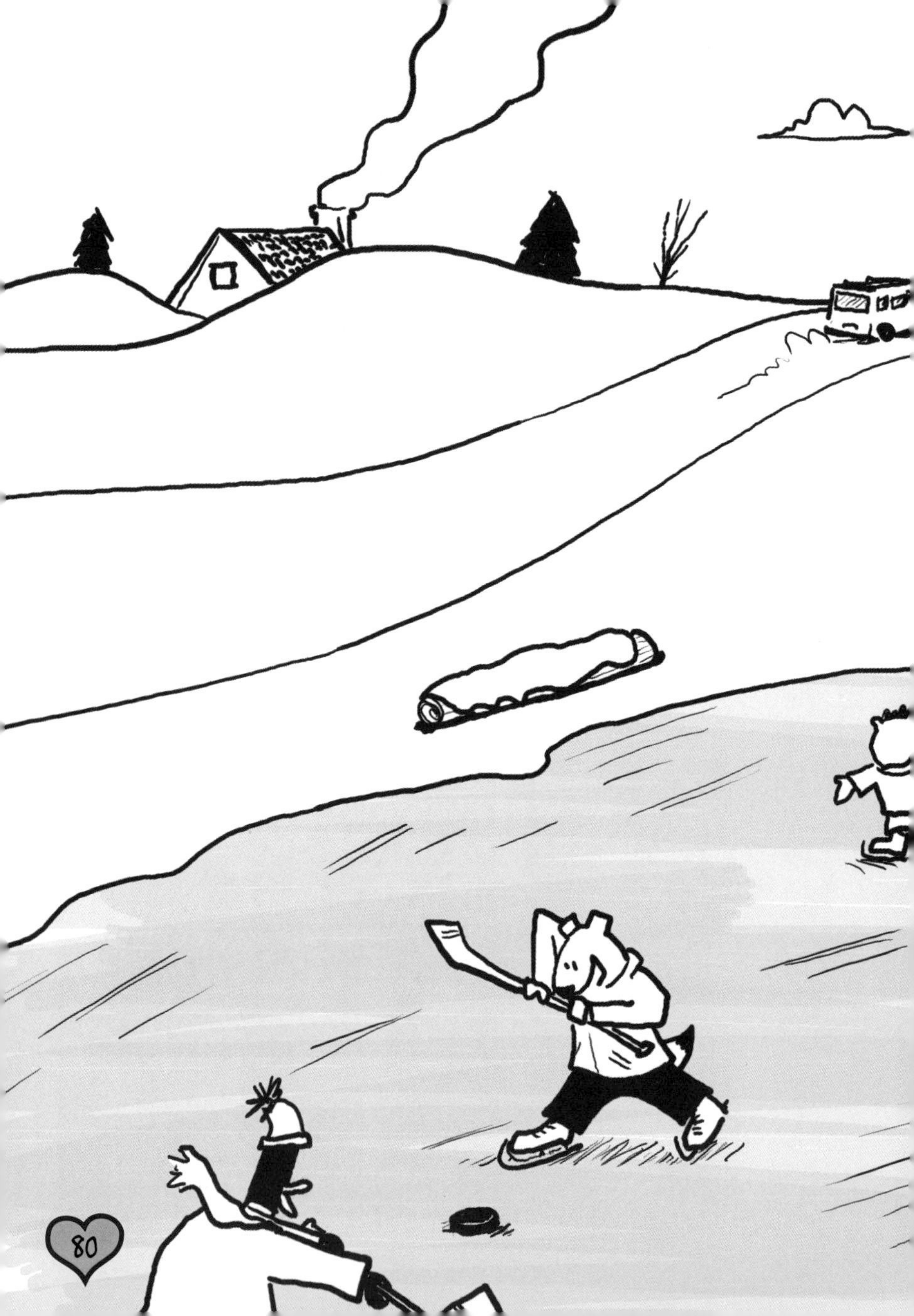

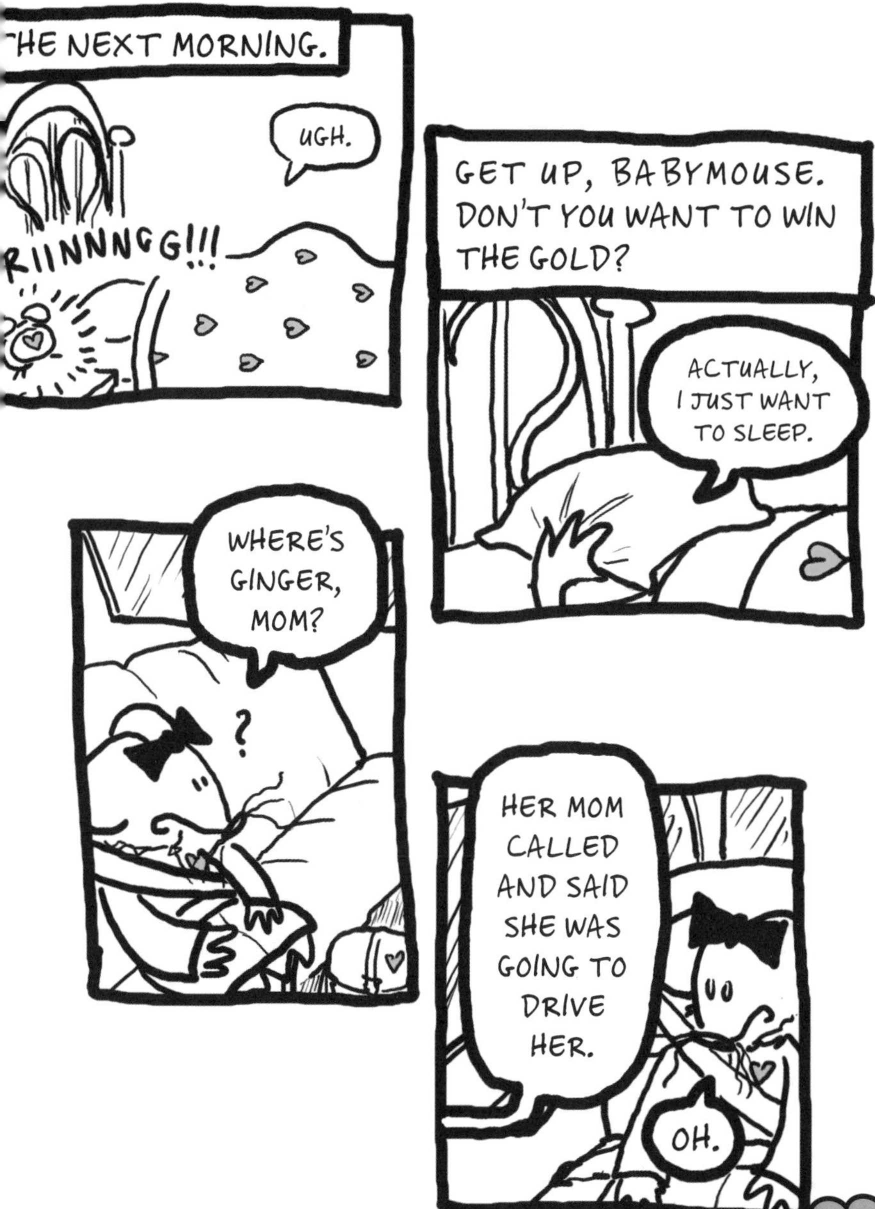
THE NEXT MORNING.
UGH.
RIIINNNGG!!!
GET UP, BABYMOUSE. DON'T YOU WANT TO WIN THE GOLD?
ACTUALLY, I JUST WANT TO SLEEP.
WHERE'S GINGER, MOM?
?
HER MOM CALLED AND SAID SHE WAS GOING TO DRIVE HER.
OH.

BECAUSE THAT'S WHAT IT TAKES TO BE A WINNER AND I AM GOING TO WIN.
BUT WINNING ISN'T EVERYTHING.
WINNING **IS** EVERYTHING! I AM GOING TO GET THAT GOLD TROPHY!
BUT, BUT, BUT, WHAT ABOUT FRIENDS AND BOOKS AND CUPCAKES AND—
FRIENDS? YOU CAN'T BE FRIENDS WITH GIRLS YOU COMPETE AGAINST. AND WHEN WOULD I HAVE TIME TO READ A **BOOK?** NOT TO MENTION I HAVEN'T TOUCHED A CUPCAKE IN **FIVE YEARS!**
YOU'RE **NOTHING** IF YOU DON'T WIN!

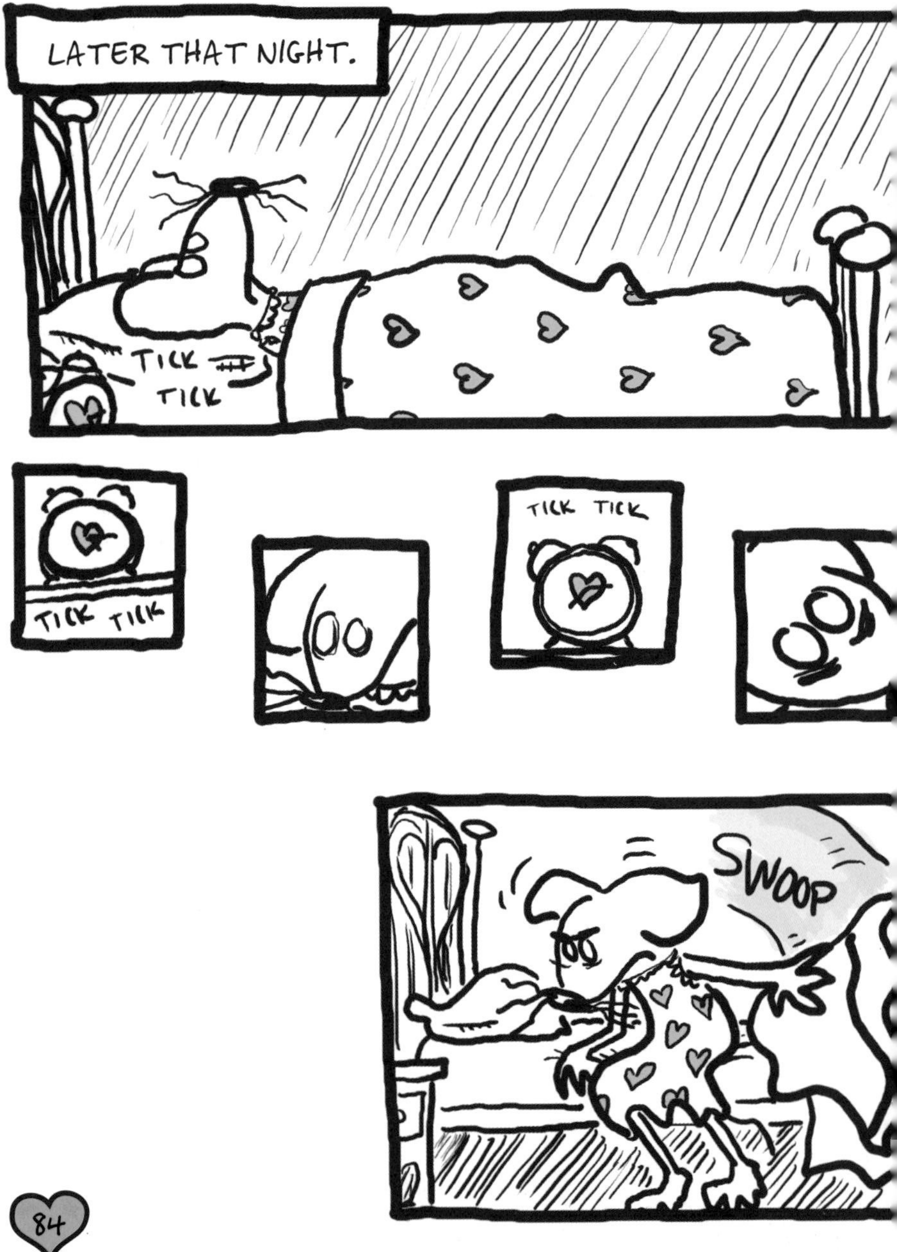
LATER THAT NIGHT.
TICK
TICK
TICK TICK
TICK TICK
SWOOP

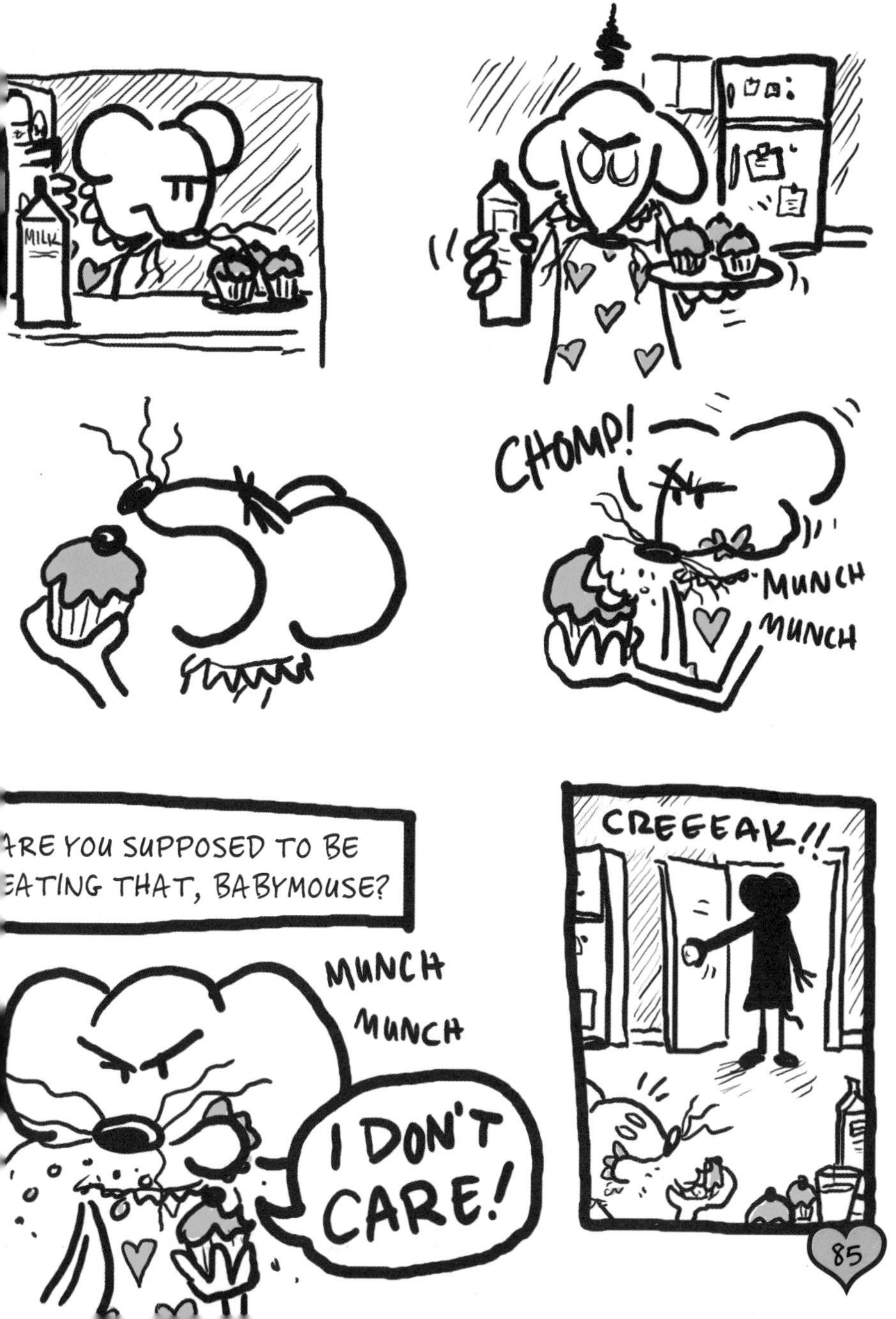
MILK
CHOMP!
MUNCH
MUNCH
ARE YOU SUPPOSED TO BE EATING THAT, BABYMOUSE?
MUNCH
MUNCH
I DON'T CARE!
CREEEAK!!

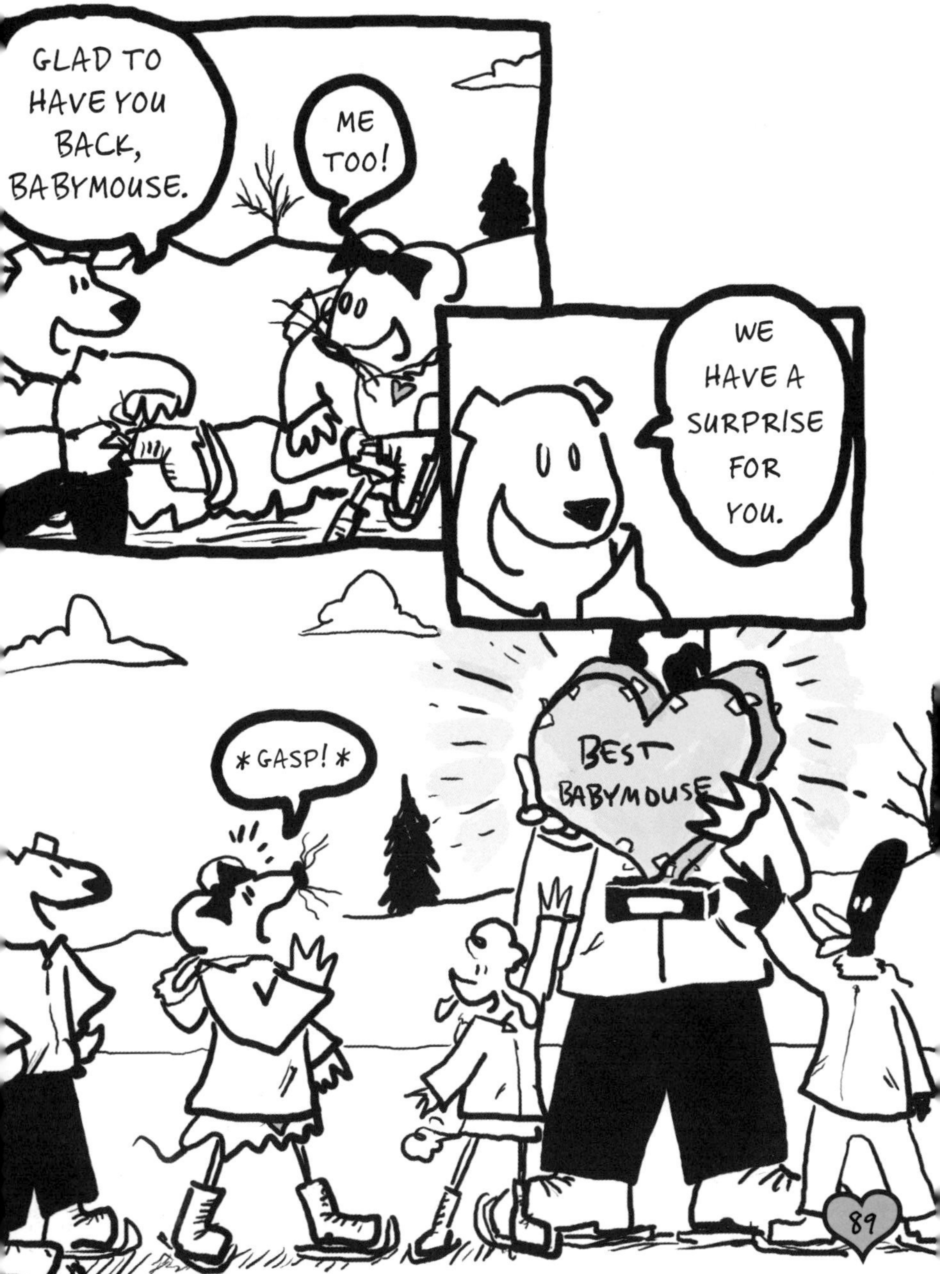
GLAD TO HAVE YOU BACK, BABYMOUSE.
ME TOO!
WE HAVE A SURPRISE FOR YOU.
GASP!
BEST BABYMOUSE

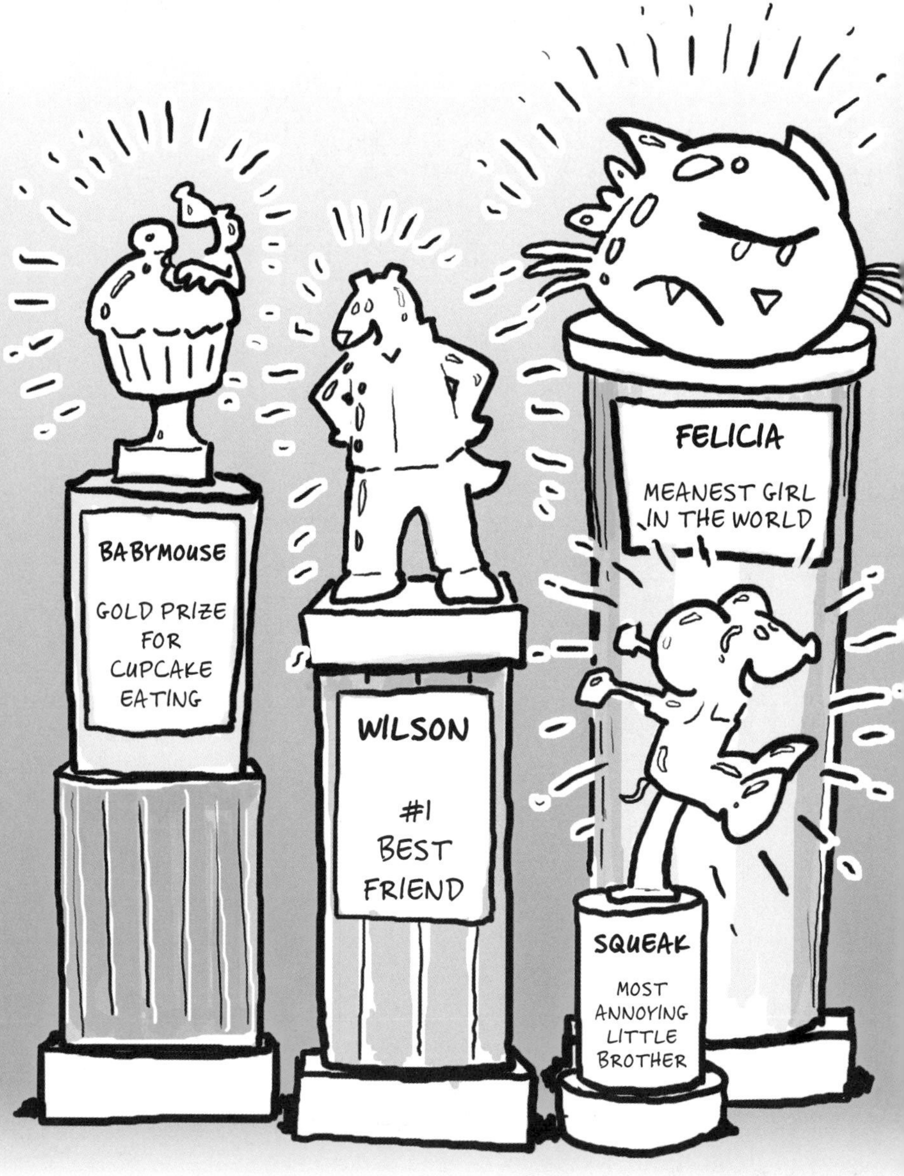
BABYMOUSE
GOLD PRIZE FOR CUPCAKE EATING
WILSON
#1 BEST FRIEND
FELICIA
MEANEST GIRL IN THE WORLD
SQUEAK
MOST ANNOYING LITTLE BROTHER